Albert Lee

Four for a Fortune

A Tale

Albert Lee

Four for a Fortune
A Tale

ISBN/EAN: 9783337026073

Printed in Europe, USA, Canada, Australia, Japan

Cover: Foto ©Andreas Hilbeck / pixelio.de

More available books at **www.hansebooks.com**

FOUR FOR A FORTUNE

A TALE. By *ALBERT LEE*

Author of "Tommy Toddles"

ILLUSTRATED By *F. C. YOHN*

NEW YORK AND LONDON
HARPER & BROTHERS PUBLISHERS
1898

CONTENTS

CONTENTS

ILLUSTRATIONS

FOUR FOR A FORTUNE

A MAJORITY *of those who read this story will set it down as fiction. They will refuse to believe that any such events as are here narrated could occur at the close of the nineteenth century without some knowledge of them coming to the authorities, and through them to the newspapers and to the public. There are some, however, under whose eyes these pages may come who will know that this is history; that everything told of, and more too, actually happened; and that only the names of individuals are changed — in some cases merely disguised. Others will find here a partial explanation of certain* strange occurrences with which they were innocently more or less connected.

Chiffard is alive and thriving, and goes about his business in New York as quietly and earnestly as if he had never stabbed a man and thrown his body into the sea. *Carquemort* (thank Heaven!) is dead, and may the Devil never send his like to earth again. Good Captain McLeod is no longer of the living; but Glen, I hear, has prospered and is married.

Thatcher looked over this manuscript before it left my hands, and although he hesitated at first over the possible results of the publication of the story, he soon came to view the situation much as I do, and he is now convinced that no one will believe in what I have written.

But let him who is not interested in brawl and battle, in the smell of the sea, in treasure-hunting and the staking of human life for gold; in treachery and hate; in perseverance and daring—let him,

I say, put this book aside. For from the moment Carquemort's mysterious, hypnotic, half-burned chart came into our lives, we were all of us swept along in an irresistible current made up of just those wretched human passions; and the tale of our adventures is but a record of their workings to the ultimate logical end.

How the chart actually came into Carquemort's possession I do not know. He said he found it in an old strongbox that had belonged to his grandfather; but in this statement he lied, as was afterwards conclusively proven—for he never had a grandfather. It is more than probable that he stole it; and if he did not murder the previous owner, the latter should be devoutly thankful and go at once to his little seaport shrine and burn three candles upon the altar of Our Lady. Yet, in whatever manner he became possessed of it, certain it is that Carquemort had the chart when we first met him one stormy night in April, in the year of our Lord 1894. As I look back upon it now, it seems the bitterest kind of irony to call that the "year of our Lord"; for if ever Satan had a year, or a portion of a year, to himself, it was that same summer of 1894. But that is a matter aside.

CHAPTER I

A DINNER AT CHIFFARD'S

IT WAS in April, 1894 (as I have said), that we met Carquemort. All the afternoon the rain had been coming down in streaks from a mass of dark, woolly clouds overhead, and humanity was soaked in discontent. Earlier in the day we had agreed, Thatcher and I, to brighten the evening with a modest meal at Chiffard's; and thus the dinner-hour found us picking our way over the glistening, puddly pavements of South Fifth Avenue towards Washington Square. Near Fourth Street we turned into a narrow doorway that broadens out into a dark, square hall—damp, stone-paved, and heavy with an odor of cooking—and entered the cheerful little French restaurant that occupies the lower floor of the dingy tenement. The two small rooms, set with a dozen white tables, were warm and well lighted; but it was a bad night for business, and only three guests had preceded us. The violinist and his wife sat in the corner as usual, and across the room was a bearded, broad-shouldered fellow who scarcely glanced up as we entered. He appeared thoroughly unconscious of any one's else presence, and punctuated his indifference with a noisy mouthing of his *pot-au-feu*.

Madame Chiffard, who was at her post behind the little marble counter, placidly hemming a new dozen of napkins, smiled benignly as the door opened before us, and exclaimed in her most gracious manner:

"*Ah, messieurs, mais vous avez choisi du bien mauvais temps pour venir nous voir !*"

Then, turning her head in the direction of the shaft where the rickety little dumb-waiter rattled incessantly in its excursions to the lower regions, she called out:

"*Philippe! Ces messieurs sont là!*"

I do not know whether we were the only *messieurs* who patronized Chiffard's, or whether Madame had in her heart a softer spot for us than for her other customers; but whenever she announced to Chiffard, who watched over the pots and kettles below, that "*ces messieurs*" were "*là,*" we could always confidently look forward to the enjoyment of an unusually well-cooked dinner. Thatcher was exceedingly jealous of this preference, and he had long ago made me promise never to bring any one to dine at Chiffard's, or even to tell my friends of the little restaurant's existence. He may have been justified in this secretiveness, for, as he explained when he exacted the promise:

"It is bad enough to sit around and

dine with a lot of newspaper men and Bohemians" (all the same, Thatcher numbered many a good friend and cherished companion among these same newspaper men and Bohemians!), "but when they take their privacy and sell it at space rates, it is time to retire from their company. There is no telling when you yourself will be taken as a subject for a Sunday special. You know how good Binetti's was, two years ago? And you remember those jolly summer evenings we used to spend at Dagorre's? Well, those fellows had to go and write about it all, didn't they? And reprint pictures stolen from the Paris weeklies to give their stories 'local color?' Bah! And now Binetti's is full of dry-goods clerks and addle-pated youths who call nightly for Chianti (which they never get!); and Dagorre's has had such a run of the herd that I would not stall my horse there—if I had one!"

Fortunately Thatcher's autocratic boycott of Bohemians and newspaper men did not seem to injure Chiffard's business. He derived a good trade from the French folk of the quarter, and prospered. One day he consulted with Thatcher about advertising in an afternoon paper. Thatcher nearly fainted at the suggestion, and forthwith painted the results of newspaper advertising in such black colors that the frugal Frenchman at once gave up all idea of ever seeing his name in print.

"The day will come soon enough," Thatcher said to me afterwards, "when Chiffard will believe himself the only restaurant-keeper who ever successfully boiled a *bouillabaisse* south of the Arch. Then he will move up into the Tenderloin, hire a place with a white-painted front and plate-glass windows—and fail!"

Thatcher was at times inclined to be cynical.

But to return to this eventful evening of the year of the Devil 1894. By the time the coffee and cheese were placed upon the table, it was near nine o'clock. It was improbable any more customers would come in. Madame stepped down from her high perch behind the counter and brought her sewing to our table, where her husband had already joined us. He wore his immaculate cook's hat on the back of his head, and the sleeves of his spotless white coat were turned well up so as to display a pair of well-developed tattooed arms, for Chiffard had served in the French Navy. He rolled cigarette after cigarette and puffed the room full of light-blue smoke, while we all talked and laughed and told stories, as you always do at Chiffard's, and drank pretty-colored, queer-named *liqueurs* out of funny little thimble-like glasses, and Thatcher said "*Sacré!*" at most inopportune moments—and altogether we had a very good time. Our conversations in the little restaurant were, of course, always carried on in French; but as this is neither a stenographic report nor a dialectic essay, I shall not attempt to reproduce the cook's wild rhetoric or Thatcher's utter disregard of the rules set down by Noël and Chaptal. The topics we discussed ranged from soup to politics, with eloquence for the former and true Gallic vehemence for the latter, for Chiffard was what Stevenson would have described as a veritable petard of a fellow, although by no means worn to skin and bone, like the host of the inn at Origny-Sainte-Benoîte. Our host was fat. His petardism was at times trying to my nerves; but Madame, who was a quiet little body herself, used to notice this; and I think she sympathized with me, for frequently, with one hand placed upon her spouse's brawny arm, she would adroitly turn the drift of the conversation from politics back again to soup.   And I was duly grateful.

On this particular rainy evening, however, the petard appeared distracted and thoughtful.   He did not talk so boisterously as of wont, and he acted as a man does whose mind is set upon another matter.   Frequently he looked over his shoulder at the bearded guest in the other room.   The fellow had finished his dinner and sat, pipe in mouth, reading the French newspapers.   The violinist and his wife had left long since, and I wondered why the stranger lingered. After a while Chiffard said:

" That man used to be a quartermaster in the French Navy."

" He looks more like a pirate," said Thatcher.

" I think he deserted," continued Chiffard.   " He does not say much about it. I knew him ten years ago on the *Cuverville*, and befriended him once."

"I suppose he wants a meal on the strength of his reminiscences," I suggested.

"No. He pays. It is not that he wants." Chiffard glanced over his shoulder again, and then leaning forward to us, he whispered: "He showed me a chart!"

This statement evidently did not impress either Thatcher or me as much as Chiffard had intended it should.

"Is there anything particularly odd about a sailor having a chart?" I asked, noticing his disappointment.

"You do not understand," whispered Chiffard again. "It is gold—it is treasure!"

"Oho!" exclaimed Thatcher, laughing. "Mr. Bunco, eh? How much did he want you to invest in the chart?"

"Ah, it is not that. He will not sell the map. He does not know where the place is. He wants me to tell him of some one who can help him to find out."

" Well, bring him over here," suggested Thatcher, "and tell him I am an authority on Captain Kidd and buried treasure and mysterious islands. Tell him I'll find the gold for him if he will give me half the spoils !"

" I fear he will not trust you Americans," said Chiffard, who seemed to take the treasure chart most seriously. " You see, he waits for you to go. He wants to come and talk to me again."

We urged Chiffard to invite the stranger to our table, and although he demurred considerably at first, he finally turned towards the man and said:

"Eh, Monsieur Carquemort ! Venez donc prendre quelque chose avec nous."

Carquemort looked up from his paper, grunted something that sounded like " *Merci bien*," and went on reading again.

" What a bear !" remarked Madame.

" You see, he will not," said Chiffard,

shrugging his shoulders. But Thatcher was not to be so easily denied. He called upon our host to go over and persuade the seaman to join us, and when Chiffard persistently objected Thatcher threatened to go and get him himself. Thereupon Chiffard rose reluctantly and went over to Carquemort and sat down beside him. They talked for several minutes in undertones.

"All that fellow needs to make him look like a genuine pirate," observed Thatcher, as we watched them, "is a red handkerchief tied around his head, a cutlass in his hand, and a brace of pistols in his belt."

I looked at him again, and could not but appreciate the force of the remark. Little did I suspect that under three months I should see this same Carquemort in practically the outfit suggested by Thatcher, standing on the deck of a vessel at sea, cursing and fighting—a real pirate in appearance and at heart, if ever there was one. The greatest blessing Divine Providence has wasted on humanity is ignorance of the future.

After ten minutes of conversation with Chiffard, Carquemort consented to accept our hospitality. When Madame saw him coming, she gathered up her napkins and bade us good-night, saying she found no pleasure in the society of the villains her husband was occasionally forced to entertain.

CHAPTER II

A HALF-BURNED CHART AND ITS STORY

THERE have been moments when I felt convinced that Carquemort possessed not a single redeeming virtue, but if only for the sake of ruining his chance to priority in hell, I must concede him one. He always came directly to the point, whatever might be the subject under discussion. This is unusual with a Frenchman, especially with a Frenchman of his class, or with any man of his nature, if his mate exists on earth unhanged. There was never any beating about the bush with Carquemort; and he had what was sometimes a most objectionable habit of calling a spade a spade.

The night of our first meeting he

pulled a chair up to the table after the formal introductions had been made, and, looking first at one of us and then at the other with his small, heavy-browed, beady eyes, he said:

"Chiffard has told you that I have a chart, and you want to see it?"

"That's about the size of it," answered Thatcher, lightly; but Carquemort glared at him in a manner which plainly showed he did not like this levity, and I realized at once we must go about it carefully if we wished the man to talk. I kicked Thatcher under the table. Then I said:

"Chiffard has told us about the chart, but not much. As I understand it, you have a map on which is designated the location of hidden treasure. Such things are always interesting, of course; but one does not run across hidden treasure very frequently nowadays, and it will require some proof to persuade us that your chart is not a *blague.* If you can do that, we may be able to aid you."

"You speak well," answered Carquemort. "Chiffard assures me that, although Americans, you are both men of honor, and that if I show you the chart you will put your knowledge of its contents to no other use but that which may be agreed to between us. As to whether it is a *blague*—it will not take you long to determine that for yourself."

He spoke as a man filled with confidence, and I admit I was impressed by his manner. We readily agreed to make no use of information we might derive from the chart, for all we wanted of it, and of him, was an evening's entertainment. Chiffard sat by in silence, leaning forward on both elbows, eagerly attentive, and Thatcher had assumed a gravity of demeanor which seemed to reassure Carquemort, and which apparently inspired him with confidence in Thatcher's integrity. He felt in the inner pocket of his double-breasted sailor-jacket and pulled out a dark-leather pocket-book, from which he took a well-worn, blue-linen envelope. From this he extracted the chart and laid it on the table.

I cannot analyze the peculiar feelings which came over me the instant I saw that piece of paper. They were a mixture of fear, greed, hope, and determination. There was no sensation of doubt, and none of joy. I have tried many times to explain to Thatcher just how I felt, and he has tried to do the same concerning himself, for me; but neither of us has been very successful. We both agree that our brains swam in a kind of feverish excitement. As for me, I was satisfied at a glance that the map was a very ancient one, and my interest was at once bound up in it. Thatcher, from scoffer, turned champion—aye, fanatic—so wonderful was the influence of that bit of

THE CHART

brown paper on him. There was something uncanny in this fascination, something weird and of the supernatural; and it was exerted over every one who ever saw the chart. I could well understand Chiffard had felt so restless and unrlier in the evening.

as a small piece of brown paper, so thick that I took it at first to be parchment. It had originally been oblong in form, about three inches by five; but when we first saw it a portion had been burned away, leaving the top and the right-hand edge of the paper charred and irregular. Across the upper portion these words, prefixed by a cross in red ink, remained of what had been written:

<pre>
X   Ici son   oooo . . .
        environ en or   pièces et . . .
</pre>

. The cross referred to a similar red mark on one of a group of islands carefully outlined in the centre of the sheet. The name of the group had evidently been written down, for near the charred edge of the paper appeared these fragments of words in capital letters:

ILE
SAI
MI

The remaining space was taken up with what appeared to be a kind of explanatory inscription, fully half of which had been destroyed in the burning. This much had been spared:

Pour trouver la cach
on se met le dos
contre le mat
l'on marche
directe ver
croix sur
chiens u
de 25 pa
la pierr
creuse

A much better conception of what the document looked like may be obtained from the picture given herewith, which is taken from a photograph of the original. But no reproduction or description can ever convey the slightest idea of the wonderful fascination the original chart itself had upon all those who saw it or who came in contact with it. Chiffard said it was bewitched, and he may be right. I used to scoff at any belief in supernatural agencies or influences; but I have gotten over that now.

We all four sat there in silence gazing at those few square inches of yellow paper, the fever burning in our pulses and our heads throbbing. Finally, Carquemort knocked the ashes out of his pipe, and this pounding on the table brought us back to our senses. Thatcher was the first to speak:

"Where are these islands?" he asked.

"I do not know," replied Carquemort.

" That is what he wants you to find out," put in Chiffard, nervously.

" But there are a good many islands in this world," said I, picking up the chart and scrutinizing it carefully; " and there is not much of a clew to the whereabouts of this particular group to be found in this map. How did it come to get burned?"

" I cannot tell," said Carquemort. " It was so when I got it."

" And where did you get it?"

He hesitated a moment, then replied: " It came to me when my grandfather died. But that is unimportant. Here is the chart. We will talk of that." His tone plainly forbade further inquiry. But I was athirst for facts.

" I don't want to ask unreasonable questions," I said, " but there are some things we must know." Carquemort's face twitched slightly, and he started to speak; but I raised my hand and shut

WE ALL GAZED IN SILENCE AT THOSE FEW SQUARE INCHES OF CHARRED PAPER

him off. "Wait a moment. We are interested in this map—very much interested, as you no doubt see. I don't care so far as you, personally, are concerned where or how you got it; but I want some explanation of how it came to light after apparently having been hidden away for so many years. Do you understand what I mean?"

"I do," said Carquemort, somewhat sullenly.

"Don't you see," I continued, persuasively, "that, unless we can satisfy ourselves that no one else has had possession of this map in a way to know its value, there is no use of our spending our time in seeking out these islands?"

"I do not believe the existence of the paper has been known of for over a hundred years," answered Carquemort, slowly, and with much apparent effort. "The paper was locked in a box. I opened the box three years ago in St. Malo. A lad read to me the writing on the paper, and I kept it without telling any one of it. The lad was much excited and deeply affected by what he read, just as you have been and as I was when he repeated it to me; but he promised to tell no one of it, and I believe he kept his word. At any rate, he had little time to speak much of it, for we sailed away on the same bark—the *Sainte Geneviève*—three days later, he as *mousse* and I as second mate."

Here Carquemort paused for a moment and inhaled a cloud of smoke.

"He was the only one besides myself who knew of the existence of the chart," he continued. "He was washed overboard one night."

He spoke in hoarse tones, and his voice grew fainter as he told the story. The last words were almost whispered as he leaned far over the table, looking at none of us, and they could not conceal the truth. I shuddered and closed my eyes, but so great an impression did the story make upon my mind that I have since frequently wakened from a sound sleep at hearing that boy's cry as he was " washed overboard " in the night.

There was another brief silence, broken at last by Thatcher.

" You can't read, then ?"

" No, sir."

" That's why you showed the map to the boy ?"

" Yes."

" And who else has seen it since ?"

" No one—until to-day. I showed it then to Chiffard."

" Why did you keep it so secret for three years ?" I interrupted, somewhat impatiently. " You said it was three years ago you got it in St. Malo, didn't you ?"

" Yes," he answered, sitting up straight and raising his voice until it sounded almost like a hoarse yell in the quiet little room. "Three years I kept it. I could not use it. There seemed to be a curse upon it. I was superstitious, perhaps." Then his voice lowered, and there was an expression of almost savage greed in the depths of his eyes. "But I must use it now. I might as well die finding the gold as die for fear of it! Ask me no more—I have answered your question. It is certain that nobody has seen this chart since it was made and hidden away, and I believe it must have been in existence a hundred years or more."

"But there is one more point upon which we must be satisfied," I insisted, "and after that we can let the past be gone. How came you here, having sailed from St. Malo three years ago?"

"The *Sainte Geneviève* was bound for Cayenne, French Guiana," proceeded Carquemort, straightforwardly, now somewhat calmed. "We had bad weather from the start, and at the end of four months were blown upon the desert island of Trinidad, off Brazil. The bark went to pieces on the rocks and two of the men died. The rest of us were taken off at the end of six weeks by a British tramp, that landed us in Buenos Ayres. The French Consul there finally put us aboard a steamer for London, but we broke down and had to put into Rio. There I left my mates and shipped on a coffee-trader for New Orleans. We lay three months at Santos (where the men were dying like flies with yellow-fever) before we could get a cargo; and when at last I got to New Orleans, a month ago, with fifty dollars in my pocket, I made up my mind that as soon as we could clear quarantine I'd come to New York and see if I could not get a change of luck. This chart is all I have, and I'm going to find these islands if I can get any help; it's the last card I have to play!"

" Well," said I, "exactly what do you wish to do if by any means we should discover the location of these islands ?"

" Go there," said Carquemort, curtly.

" But that will cost money," said Thatcher.

" I furnish the chart ; you furnish the money."

" And then what ?" I asked.

" About the treasure ?"

" Yes."

" We divide."

" If we furnish money enough to get to these islands—wherever they may be —and find the treasure, you will share equally with us anything that may be unearthed ?"

" I will agree to that," said Carquemort.

" I should like to think this over a little," I said, in an undertone, turning to Thatcher.

" Of course," he replied ; " but I wanted

to know what kind of a deal he was willing to make."

"And me?" exclaimed the cook, anxiously—"and me? Where am I in here?"

"We shall have to see about that, Chiffard," answered Thatcher, smiling. "We will dine here again to-morrow night, and then perhaps we can talk more seriously about this."

"That is all very well," said I; "but how can we talk about it if we don't know where the islands are? How is that to be learned?" And I turned inquiringly towards Carquemort.

He shrugged his shoulders after the fashion of his race, and asked if there was not enough written on the chart to show where the treasure was hidden. He seemed incredulous when we told him that there were only a few letters that gave the slightest clew to the identity of the islands.

"But there may be enough," added

Thatcher; "and after we have set to work in earnest we may be able to decipher the enigma. I don't intend to throw up my hands yet." I had never seen him so enthusiastic.

It was some time before we could persuade Carquemort to let us have a copy of the chart; but we finally convinced him that no harm could possibly come of it, and that we must have some such data to aid us in working out the problem that must be solved before any further steps could be taken. And so, after the map and the writing had been carefully traced upon a thin sheet of paper, Carquemort put the precious documents away in his pocket again, and we parted for the night.

CHAPTER III

INVESTIGATION AND SPECULATION

IT was late when we left Chiffard's. The rain had ceased, and as we walked slowly homeward over the dappled pavements we discussed the unusual events of the evening. We both frankly admitted to each other being deeply affected by what we had seen and heard, and neither concealed his anxiety to get to work at the deciphering of the mysterious chart—an undertaking which must—now—seem to any sane person an absolutely impossible task. But the sane person is not under the influence which overpowered us at that time.

" Let us be systematic, and, at least, begin at the beginning," I suggested, as we laid the tracing out on the table. "The first sentence we find somewhat the worse for wear, but what there is of it is plain enough:

> "Ici son   oooo . . .
> environ en or   pièces et . . ."

"That doesn't look over-promising, does it?" said Thatcher. "But it is plain that *son* was originally *sont*."

"Plain as day. *Ici sont*—here are; or, in the words of the head-stones, ' here lie.'"

" Four zeros."

" That must have been at the very least 10000," I said.

" Fully that. I don't see how it could have been less. You are conservative."

" My real opinion, however, is that the total figure represented a larger sum."

" There is certainly room enough for more figures on that line," said Thatcher, laughing.

" Oh yes; but you've got to put a word

WE WALKED SLOWLY HOMEWARD

in between *sont* and the zeros—*enterrés*, or *cachés*, or *déposés*, or something equivalent."

"But even the longest one of those words would leave plenty of space for more figures." And we went at our problem with a millimetre measure, gauging the spread of the chart-maker's chirography. But of course it all came to naught, and we presently abandoned that investigation and took up the second line, "*environ en or pièces et . . .*"

"It looks as if there might have been another word after those zeros," said Thatcher.

"There's certainly something lacking in the sentence as it stands. Suppose the first missing word were 'hidden.' Then it would read, '*Ici sont cachés . . . oooo . . . environ en or pièces et . . .*' I think there ought to be some punctuation after *or*, say a comma or a dash; '*pièces et*' and whatever followed were explanatory of the gold; don't you think so? *Pièces* means coin—pieces of money. Evidently the treasure is in coin and bullion, or ingots, eh? Ingots is a good old pirate word; *pièces et lingots.* How's that?"

" Make it *pièces et lingots* for the present. But how about the word following the zeros?"

After a good deal of debate and thought, it struck us that this word must have been some expression of monetary value—such as francs, pounds, ducats, doubloons, or Louis d'or; and this seemed reasonable, since it would have been only natural for the writer of the map to designate in some way the value of his buried hoard. So we gave up speculating upon that sentence and turned to the consideration of the eight capital letters that stood below, near the outline of the islands, and, after a brief examination, we concluded that these fragments

ILE

SAI

MI

must represent the name of the group.
We determined, at any rate, to proceed
on this basis, and should our premises
prove false, we could but begin over again.

"*ILE* is certainly the French for isl-
and," said Thatcher, writing the letters
out on a pad.

" It was probably written *ILES*," said
I, "in the plural, for you see there are
more islands than one shown on the map,
and the last letter has no doubt been
burned off. Let us take that for granted—we have got to take a lot for granted
in this search, so it matters little where
we begin. Now here we have *ILES
SAI . . . MI . . .*"

" Exactly," returned Thatcher. " Now,
the main question is, Where are the *Iles
Sai . . . Mi . . . ?*"

" By Jericho!" I exclaimed, jumping to

my feet, " I have it!   It's as plain as day!
The *S-A-I* stands for *Saint*.   They are
the Isles of Saint something."

" Certainly!" shouted Thatcher, now
very much excited; "that's it precisely.
Saint Michael, eh?—or, rather, *Saint
Michel.*"

" Are there any *Iles Saint Michel?*" I
asked, trembling with excitement.

" Oh, there must be!" gasped Thatcher
—"there must be! The French have
islands and towns for every saint on the
calendar."

" They probably have," I continued,
more calmly; "but Michael surely has
not a monopoly on the initial letters M I.
There may be any number of saints
whose names begin with those letters."

" How shall we find out?"

" One way is to get a gazetteer or a geo-
graphical dictionary, and write out a list
of all the islands whose names begin with
Saint Mi . . ."

" That's it," interrupted Thatcher, gleefully; " and then we'll get a map and look up each one until we find the group that corresponds in outline and general configuration with the one sketched on the chart. My boy, my boy, have a million with me!"

It took us much longer, of course, to arrive at these conclusions than I have here set down, but having reached them in approximately that line of reasoning, we felt satisfied with our achievement, and brought down the stocky bottle of King William from the top shelf and built castles so high and so late that the dawn crept in through the windows and gilded their mythical battlements before we parted, promising to meet a few hours later in the Astor Library.

Here we encountered our first disappointment, as I had had a vague fear we should, as the gazetteer was replete with names of saintly islands that began with the letters M I. There were Saint Michaels, Saint Michels, Saint Mihiels, Saint Miguels, and Saint Miniatos without number.

" Well," observed Thatcher, sadly, "it's a case of take-your-choice, I suppose."

" It's a case of work," I answered. "The process of elimination will be a long one, but it must be thoroughly done. Get an atlas."

While Thatcher was making life a burden to the librarian in his attempt to get maps of the world on the largest possible scale, I wrote down one beneath the other, in a long list, the names of the islands that might hold our secret. When completed, there were over thirty on the list, the most promising being the islands of Saint Michael in the Azores, Saint Michael in Cornwall, and Saint Michael off the coast of Labrador. We patiently searched out each individual isle and each group separately, and compared them with our tracing of Carquemort's chart, but not one corresponded in any way. Then we made a second and a third comparison, and at the end we had not even a hope left that the chart-maker had been a poor draftsman, and had only roughly outlined the spot where his treasure lay. There was no group of four islands with a name beginning " Saint Mi."

" Well," sighed Thatcher—and his face wore a look of disappointment that was pathetic—"there is one thing left. We can go through these atlases and compare our chart with every group of islands in the world."

" That would be nonsense," I replied, "and no one but a crazy man would think of such a thing."

" I don't pretend to be anything else but a crazy man now," he said.

" In the first place, that atlas or any other does not show all the islands of the world. It could not. There are millions of islands. Every river, every bay, every shore is dotted with islands. Many are not shown on any map. It is more than likely that this treasure is laid away in some obscure group that used to be frequented by pirates and sea-robbers. I don't know what we can do."

"I know what we won't do," retorted Thatcher; "we won't give up—not just yet, at least. If you think the stuff is hidden on an island that used to be frequented by pirates, I am willing to investigate all the West Indian groups and all the Louisiana and Florida islands."

"Investigate?" I exclaimed.

"Not personally," said Thatcher. "I am not as mad as that. But I'll stay here all day and go over every map I can lay hold of. I shall then at least have the satisfaction of knowing where the islands are *not*, even if I don't locate them."

I could not stay with him, because I had an appointment down town. I would not have stayed with him if I could. I considered his scheme rank lunacy, and told him so; but Thatcher was not to be dissuaded. He was an individual of unlimited determination and spasmodic perseverance. If this latter quality had been fixed in him, Thatcher would have been a genius. So I left him with his atlases, agreeing to meet him in the evening at Chiffard's, and promising to fill out in the meanwhile, if I could, the half-burned inscription on the lower part of the chart, which neither of us had attempted to decipher as yet.

CHAPTER IV

DEDUCTIONS AND CONCLUSIONS

THE labor I had so cheerfully assumed proved no easy task, as I very soon discovered, and I spent three hours of the afternoon in partially piecing out the lines where the words had been burned away. I did not expect to make any important discovery by doing this, but I wanted to have some results to show Carquemort at dinner-time. The broken sentence, as it appeared on my copy of the chart, ran thus:

> Pour trouver la cach
> on se met le dos
> contre le mat
> l'on marche
> directe ver
> croix sur ·

chiens u
de 25 pa
la pierr
creuse

The result of my labors was not re-markably satisfactory, but when the time came to start for Chiffard's, I had arranged the sentence in this fashion:

Pour trouver la cach*ette*
on se met le dos
contre le mat *et* (?)
l'on marche *en ligne* (?)
directe ver*s la*
croix sur
chiens u
de 25 pa*s*
la pierr*e*
creuse

To be sure, I had added but a few let-ters, yet I felt that, little as this was, I had accomplished something. There could be no doubt that *cachette* was the word indi-cated by *cach*, or that *ver* had been *vers*, *pa* had been *pas*, and *pierr* must have been *pierre*. I did not feel so sure about the insertion of the words *en ligne* at the end of the fourth line, or the article *la* at the end of the fifth; but they made sense, and that was something, for further along I could not make any sense at all. Translated, my revised version read: "To find the hiding-place, put your back against the mast and walk in a straight line directly towards the cross on . . . dogs . . . 25 steps . . . the stone . . . dig."

The first part of this, of course, was plain—that is, it was plain in so far as, by locating the hiding-place, it confirmed in a measure the statement, made in the words at the top of the chart, that there was treasure concealed somewhere on the island. But then, again, it was not plain at all, for the directions were exceedingly vague, and I could not help recalling the old fable of the three wise men who rowed to the middle of the lake and there threw a bag of gold overboard, marking the spot for future identification by cutting a notch in the side of their boat. My map-maker had apparently located the *cachette* on the island by standing with his back to the mast of his ship, and Heaven only knows where the ship was anchored or how the tide ran at the time he took his bearings. This was grievously discouraging. And as to what "the cross," "dogs," "25 steps," and "stone" might mean I could not dream. As I walked through Washington Square and let the cool evening breeze blow across my feverish forehead, I wondered, in a confused, irrational sort of way, if the witless chart-maker had taken his line from the "mast" of a ship at sea to a "cross" on shore, where there was a pack of "dogs" standing "25 steps" from some "stone." If such were the case, even with the island found, we should have a merry time searching for the spot to "dig" for the *cachette.*   What bitter, bitter irony to invite us to dig on such slim, idiotic, worse than useless directions!

On arriving at the little restaurant in South Fifth Avenue, I found Thatcher and Carquemort already at table. So solemn looked Thatcher that there was no necessity for him to tell me his search among the West Indian islands had been fruitless; but it was nevertheless pleasing to hear him report his failure for the mere sake of enjoying the picturesqueness of his profanity. Carquemort had been sipping absinthe all the afternoon—so Chiffard told us later—and was in sullen mood. He was inclined to be querulous, wherefore Thatcher, whose temper had not been improved by his afternoon's experience, ordered him to be quiet and bade him dine, that he might be the better possessed of his senses when Chiffard should join us later.

Madame was as cordial as ever, and her

cheery announcement to her spouse of "*ces messieurs sont là*" rang out clearly through the room, bringing to me an assurance of gastronomic consolation at least. But the accursed chart had played sad havoc with Chiffard's nerves, which, in turn, had affected his culinary prowess, for I think he never cooked a worse dinner in his life.

The editing of the burned portion of the chart, insignificant as it was, seemed to give the greatest gratification to Carque-mort. He lost every vestige of sullenness in his examination of my writing, which he could not any more read than if it had been Syriac, and he displayed in the subsequent discussion an amount of intelligence and reasoning power of which his previous manner had not led us to believe him capable. His chief contribution towards the unravelling of the fragmentary directions was of greater importance than it appears as here set down. I was reviling the maker of the chart, to a soft obbligato of blasphemy and profanity by Thatcher, dwelling particularly upon the fact that the main point of direction, being taken from a movable object, was absolutely useless, when Carquemort remarked:

" You may not be right. It is possible that the mast was not on a ship."

" Oh, of course," I exclaimed, petulantly, " they may have unstepped their mast and stuck it in the sand, and they may have chained their dogs to the stone ; but, confound it, all that is not probable."

" You do not comprehend," objected Carquemort. " The word *mat* in French means just as much a pole on land as a mast on a vessel. A flag-pole is a *mat*. Did you never see a *mat de cocagne?*"

Of course I had seen a *mat de cocagne*, and many a time. I had climbed one at the Fête de Neuilly in the good old days of my Franco-American infancy, and I wondered I had not recognized all along the amphibiousness of the term. Yet there was consolation in the fact that in days of old wiser heads than mine had failed at the egg trick until Mr. C. Columbus came along. And so Carquemort was our Columbus, and the foggy atmosphere of mystery over those directions became partially cleared away. How simple the sentence now appeared: "To find the hiding-place, put your back against the pole and walk in a straight line directly towards the cross on . . . dogs . . . 25 steps . . . the stone . . . dig."

"But confound the cross on the dogs!" exclaimed Thatcher. "What on earth can be the connection between the dogs and the cross?"

"There must be some connection," I said. "And yet there is not room for more than one or two words at the end of that line. We shall have to find out what they are before we can go much further."

And so we puzzled and puzzled, but our labors bore no fruit; and we parted again, weary and mentally chafing, hoping against hope, but ever strong in our belief that in the end we must succeed. As the cynical Thatcher put it, this was a missing-word contest, limited to four competitors, with a prize of untold sums in gold. And so we kept on guessing.

CHAPTER V

THE FINGER OF FATE

FOR many days we made no progress whatever, and almost every evening we dined at Chiffard's. Madame made little pretence of concealing the fact that she looked upon us as weak-minded visionaries, and she often rated her husband severely. But the petard took this censure meekly, as usual, and reserved his explosions for Carquemort, whose funds were rapidly ebbing low, and who now threatened to become a charge upon his old shipmate of the *Cuverville*. This serious feature of the situation first appealed to Thatcher. He had overheard a conversation between the two, and, being a man of action and expedient, he forthwith asked Carquemort why he did not find work.

" I am only fit for the sea," he replied, somewhat sullenly.

" It is better to work on land than to starve," said Thatcher, sharply; and he followed up the rebuke by offering to get him a place down town somewhere.

" What is the good?" retorted Carquemort. " I speak but few words of English—'Thank you,' 'How much?' 'Goddam!'—and I should be of no use to journalists, except perhaps to furnish them with lies."

Chiffard, for some reason, had concluded that Thatcher and I earned our living by the pen. He always spoke of us as "*ces messieurs les journalistes.*" It was of no importance to him, of course, whether we journalized daily or merely incidentally. In his eyes we were members of that vast craft which he believed could make or unmake any condition of affairs, and consequently we commanded his admiration. It was for this reason, we afterwards learned, that he urged Carquemort to take us into his confidence. Chiffard felt sure we could help the man, or that if we could not, we had the means of reaching others who might be able to. As a matter of fact, neither of us was in any way connected with journalism. Thatcher earned his daily bread in the manufacture and sale of leather. His father had grown rich in the Swamp, and had insisted that his son, upon graduation from college, should spend a certain number of hours daily in the shadows of the great arches of the Bridge. Thatcher was a good business man, as business men go, but he did not relish the odor of leather. He unfortunately got printers' ink on his fingers at New Haven, and printers' ink is a bacillus which, when once inoculated into the blood, can never be purged from the system.

Thatcher, however, did not neglect his duties for all that, and while he wrote occasionally, and spent much more of his time with men of Bohemian instinct than he did at the Hide and Leather Club, where the members' shoes fairly creaked with quotations, he never considered himself in any sense of the word a man of letters. He used to refer to himself as a "rank outsider, worshipping at the shrine of the Muses, with his feet mired from traffic in the Swamp."

As for myself, I had not been connected with a newspaper for eight years when we fell foul of Carquemort, although I had never let my pen grow rusty.

Thus it was that although Carquemort could truly be of no service in literature, he might prove useful in leather, and Thatcher persuaded him to take a place, temporarily at least, as porter in the house of Thatcher & Co., Cliff Street. This was cheering news to Chiffard; it was profitable for Carquemort, and in the end the seaman proved serviceable in his adopted sphere in spite of occasional surliness brought on by bad whiskey, which the truckmen of the Swamp soon taught him to like.

Carquemort's humiliating career as a landsman, however, did not last long. I believe he served the house of Thatcher & Co. just three weeks in all, and then that moment came which formed an epoch in the lives of all four of us, and which I look upon as the second nail in the coffin that this entire treasure-hunting incident ought to be buried in. The moment was that in which we substantiated the mystery of Carquemort's chart. It came about more or less accidentally, as all discoveries do, no matter how great and painstaking the preliminary labors of the finite mind may have been.

It is with no desire for taking any credit upon myself, but for the sake of making my story complete, that I give the incident of discovery in detail.   It happened on a Sunday afternoon in June.   We had been puzzling over the half-burned sentence for an hour or more, just as we had puzzled over it for days and days previously, and with no better success; and Thatcher had embroidered his conversation with more than his usual allowance of anathemas for the chart and the man who burned it. The knotty problem we had never been able to solve was the connection between *croix* and *chiens*, but on this day these words became the key to the whole situation.

"We have gone over this so many times," I was saying to him, "that I am sick of it.   I am beginning to feel that even millions would scarcely be sufficient wage for the gray matter I am daily wasting in this investigation; but I am willing to keep at it a little longer, only I am going at the thing now in a different way."

" I am glad you have found a new way," commented Thatcher, somewhat hopelessly. " What is it?"

"It is this," I went on. " We have made sense out of the words up to a point where the cross gets mixed up with the dogs. Now let us get every bit of sense and make every kind of deduction we can from what is left. It really does not make much difference what we deduce or how extravagant we are; it is better than merely staring at the chart."

" Go ahead," grunted Thatcher.

" We know, in the first place, that there is an island—in fact, several islands, but we are only interested in one of them. We know that somewhere on this particular island there is (or was) a pole or mast, possibly a flag-staff. We know further that there is also on the island a hiding-place, possibly a cave, more likely a hole, because the word *creuse* implies that, the hiding-place once found, we must dig.

We know, too, that there is a cross on the island, and possibly there are dogs. The cross is the point at which we first stick."

" And where we have stuck for a month," said Thatcher.

" Well, then, let us see what we can do with that cross. It was evidently a land-mark, or the writer of the chart could not, and probably would not, have used it as a basic point. It may be a cross on a church, or it may be stuck up in the ground. It must certainly have been in plain sight when these words were writ-ten. So it seems to me we want to look for an island where there is a church or a cross."

" There is probably a cross on every inhabited civilized island," said Thatcher.

" That is possible; but don't look at it from such a discouraging stand-point. Let us rather see if we cannot deduce something further from the cross."

"You have deduced a church," observed Thatcher.

"Yes, I have deduced a church. A church with a cross on it would presumably be a Catholic church. Therefore the church is in a Catholic community, and if we accept that deduction we bar out all desert islands and all islands in strictly Protestant countries."

"For the sake of argument, let it go at that," said Thatcher. "But suppose the cross is not on a church. You started by saying it might be on a steeple, or it might be sticking up out of the ground."

"If it were an isolated cross stuck into the ground, it must surely be in a Catholic country," I argued. "I remember distinctly a great crucifix on top of the cliffs at Tréport, where I spent one summer as a boy. It stands high above the village, facing seaward, and the fishermen look to it as a sort of mute guardian of their interests. Now that I think of it, it seems to me I never was in a French seaport town that did not have such a crucifix standing on some conspicuous height overlooking the harbor and the sea."

"Then you deduce from that," said Thatcher, somewhat ironically, "that on one of the islands is located a French seaport town, with a tall crucifix overlooking the sea?"

"That is not so very illogical," I answered, calmly; and I felt a peculiar thrill rising within me.

"It is not impossible, of course," resumed Thatcher, more seriously. "It is a new line for us to work on, at any rate. And, after all, why should not this be a French island? The chart is French; the writing on it is French. I wonder we did not think of this before!"

He seemed to become suddenly affected by the excitement that was brewing in me. He rose hurriedly from his chair and leaned over the tracing of the map that lay on the table.

"By gad!" he cried, "we may have struck it at last! Let's go somewhere!"

"Go somewhere?" I repeated. "Where? Where can we go to-day? It is Sunday. Libraries, like saloons, are closed on Sunday in New York. We'll have to wait until to-morrow. How foolish, after all, to get so excited over this now!"

"Excited? I have not been myself since I first saw that chart!" cried Thatcher. "Come! it's French. Let's go to some French place. We might find somebody who knows. Let's go to the Martin." And before I could realize it, Thatcher had his hat and coat on and had started down the stairs.

I followed him, and in a few moments we were at the Hôtel Martin. It is a quiet place of a Sunday, with the shades pulled well down, and peculiar - looking, bearded Frenchmen, *endimanchés*, sitting about at the marble-topped tables of the café absorbing rainbow drinks. We sat with the rest, and Thatcher asked the waiter if he did not have some sort of a directory of French towns and cities that we could look at. The waiter said there was indeed such a book, but it was chained to the desk in the office. So we perforce sought the book, inasmuch as it could not be brought to us, and we found it to be exactly what we could have wished for. It was a directory of France and of all her colonies, with maps of the Republic's foreign possessions and diagrams of many of the principal cities.

I shall not dwell upon the excitement of the moments we spent in looking through that thick, canvas-bound volume. We were as famished ones who sought for stray crumbs that might have rested between the leaves; and when we had come to the end of our search, having found nothing along the line of our in-

"WE HAVE STRUCK IT AT LAST!" HE CRIED

vestigation, we closed the big book resignedly, and the chain rattled disconsolately against the wall. Thatcher went across the room and gazed out of the window into the silent street, and I stood leaning on the desk in despair. After a few moments, in a purely mechanical way, I began fingering the leaves again, and looking at the maps and reading the curious French names; and soon I came to a picture of a group of islands in almost every respect like any other picture in the book, and I paid no attention to the name printed in big letters at the top of the page; but my eye caught, and held, as an anchor fastens to the rocky sea-bed, upon the words "*Ile aux Chiens*." Then I looked again, and I saw that the group was an enlarged counterpart of Carquemort's chart, and the name of the place as printed in the book was "*Iles Saint Pierre Miquelon*."

At the top of my voice I shouted, and

Thatcher rushed to my side and savagely seized the book, so that the chain snapped from its fastening; and in our bewilderment we dropped the volume, and it was seconds before we could find the place again.

Well, briefly, we had discovered the group we were looking for. The islands of St. Pierre Miquelon, off the south coast of Newfoundland, in longitude 56° 20′ west and latitude 47° 4′ north, were the ones traced on the chart, and across each islet of the four was written its name— St. Pierre, Grande Miquelon, Petite Miquelon, Ile aux Chiens—and the word *Chiens* was no longer a mystery and a stumbling-block. It did not now take us long to fill in the words that had been destroyed in the burning of Carquemort's paper, and here is what we made out, the italics being our additions:

Pour trouver la cach*ette*
on se met le dos

> contre le mat *et*
> l'on marche *en ligne*
> directe ver*s la*
> croix sur *l'île aux*
> chiens u*ne distance*
> de 25 pa*s*
> la pierr*e*
> creuse

The name of the group we set down on our paper thus:

> ILE*S*
> SAI*NT PIERRE*
> MI*QUELON,*

and gurgled hysterically at the reminiscence of our past futile efforts.

There was high revelry at Chiffard's that Sunday evening, and I have never seen man so drunk as Carquemort. Madame left us early, and Chiffard put up the shutters and turned the key on the public, revelling himself with his allies in the little dining-room. There was a vast amount of words wasted that night to small profit in the morning, and much good liquor sunk beneath palates that were numb to discrimination.

CHAPTER VI

A PECULIAR PARTNERSHIP

It was now July, a favorable season for a voyage to the North, and we solaced ourselves with the reflection that even if the chart and the gold and all the rest of it were a hoax, the trip to the islands might alone be worth the candle. The colony of St. Pierre Miquelon has a name for loneliness and barrenness, and Thatcher felt that if the quest proved futile, and if all else went awry, he could at least find some secluded spot up there where he might soundly thrash Carquemort; and, next to finding the gold, to thrash Carquemort seemed to be Thatcher's chief desire.

Our preparations were rapidly and easily made. There was nothing to keep me in town, and Thatcher found little trouble in arranging for a more or less indefinite absence from the leather business during the dull summer months. Carquemort, of course, had no other object in life; but with poor Chiffard it was another matter. He had to go through a stormy session with Madame before he felt certain of his plans, and even so he secured her final indorsement only by deeding to her what small property he had, and by withdrawing all his savings from the bank and turning them over to his wife. This money she took and at once deposited in another savings-bank, in her own name, and thereupon called her husband again a fool, and vowed that if he still wished to go upon the career of a wild ass and have himself shipwrecked, or, at best, waste his time instead of attending to his legitimate and proper business, which was to make the cooking in their little basement, he was free to do so, for all of her, and the sooner he rid the place of the *canaille* that had caused all the trouble the better would she be pleased. As for ourselves, we were glad that Chiffard was so anxious to go along, for we felt sure of his devotion, and welcomed it as a counterpoise to an unstable confidence in Carquemort; and, besides, as Thatcher aptly put it, it is never inconvenient to have a good cook at hand.

It had been agreed among us before we separated on that riotous Sunday night— or Monday morning, more likely — that Thatcher and I should make such arrangements as we thought best for our voyage. We had anticipated no difficulty here, but we soon discovered that there was not a steamship man or a ticket-agent in all New York who could tell us exactly, or even approximately, how to reach St. Pierre. Even at Cook's they had never heard of the place, and the clerk we questioned stared at us as if he believed we were daft when we told him we wanted to make a pleasure trip in that direction. He almost insisted upon selling us tickets to St. Pierre Martinique!

Finally it occurred to Thatcher, the planner of the quartet, that inasmuch as we had gotten our initial information at the Martin, we might secure even more from the same quarter, should we go about it in a calmer and more leisurely manner than we had on our last visit to the little hotel in University Place. And again Thatcher was right. We found a man in the café who had once heard of St. Pierre Miquelon, and he *saperlotte*-ed volubly at the reminiscence. From him we learned that the first step in our journey was to Halifax, whence frequent steamers sail for Newfoundland, and some of these, our friend thought, stopped occasionally at the French islands.

That was the best we could do, and accordingly, the four of us — Thatcher,

Carquemort, Chiffard, and I—set off from New York for Nova Scotia on Monday morning, July 22, 1894.

The last few days preceding our departure had been spent in drawing up certain legal documents, and these were signed on Saturday afternoon, the 20th—Carquemort making an anchor as his mark. There were four papers, and each of us adventurers and treasure-hunters retained a copy. The gist of the formality was to the effect that one Carquemort, seaman, of St. Malo, France, being the rightful owner and possessor of a certain chart, which apparently designated the location of hidden treasure, agreed to take the three other parties to the indenture into partnership for the purpose of obtaining and securing the said treasure. Thatcher and I bound ourselves to advance money, up to a certain amount, with which to pay the expenses of the expedition — this advance to be repaid from whatever treasure might be found. After the settling of this obligation, and the payment of all further and necessary expenses, it was stipulated that the remainder of the treasure should be divided equally among the four.

It is plain that Thatcher and I were taking the major risk in this venture; but we had talked the matter over pretty carefully before we made the proposition, and the amount we agreed to advance was but little more than the sum of what the two of us had spent during a six weeks' vacation, hunting in Colorado, the previous year. In this manner we soothed our consciences and drugged our doubts, and we juggled figures to deceive our saner instincts. Chiffard's contribution to the partnership may, at first thought, seem inconsequential and not sufficient to entitle him to a quarter-share in the proceeds. But it should be remembered that he was staking more than any other one of us—not even excepting Carquemort; and, further, we proposed to arrange things later so that he should fairly earn his salt.

My desire, from the start, had been to charter a schooner in New York, or Boston, or, better still, Gloucester, the home of the bank fishermen, and sail forth upon the seas towards the rocky shores of the treasure-holding islets, like genuine buccaneers, with Carquemort as one of the crew and Chiffard as steward. Both were seamen born and bred, and I'll wager no better cook ever stood in a galley. But Thatcher objected. He was seething with impatience, and the bare thought of calms and head winds thrust his influence in favor of the railroad—as far as Halifax, at least.

There, perhaps, he would be willing to think of taking a schooner and of giving Chiffard a chance to make himself useful.

And as I was somewhat impatient myself and not over anxious to dwell too many days on what, at best, must be a small boat, I did not stand out any too strongly for my original buccaneering proposition. It is possibly just as well, too, that I did not.

CHAPTER VII

A MOVE IN THE RIGHT DIRECTION

WE arrived at Halifax on the 24th of July, and my first impressions of the city are still somewhat confused. They consist mainly of a swarm of howling hackmen, and of a long, narrow street that runs apparently straight up into the air, the houses on either side clinging to the sidewalks by some incomprehensible evasion of the laws of gravity, doubtless peculiar to the locality. We struggled up this painfully steep street, Chiffard bending under the weight of our valises (which were certainly not included in the dispensation that seemed to favor the houses), and found our way to a comfortable hostelry, where we rested and were refreshed. Our Frenchmen we sent to an humble lodging. Rid of their encumbrance, we breathed more easily, and set out to walk about the town in quest of such knowledge as the Nova Scotians might have to offer.

It was early afternoon and the streets were thronged—so many soldiers I had not seen in one day for years—and in our delight over the novelty of the sights of a foreign city, we set our hopes and anxieties momentarily behind us and enjoyed life to its fullest extent. Thatcher, especially, seemed to delight in the red coats and the pacing sentries, and he kept impressing upon me that these were genuine soldiers—his antipathy being the militia. We met Mr. Tommy Atkins on every block, and a fine-looking young fellow he was—with his clear complexion, his broad shoulders well displayed in his scarlet tunic, his lozenge - shaped Scotch cap cocked jauntily over his right ear, and his short bamboo swagger-stick swinging loosely in his gloved hand! He looked neat and clean, too, and bore himself as if he were not ashamed of his calling and were proud of the Queen's uniform. And, walking arm in arm with him, or with a blue-jacket from the harbor, went the heavy-artillery man, clanking along the narrow pavement with sabre and spurs, gaudy in red and yellow trappings, and comical with his pill-box cap set at a thrilling angle. The first hour of this sort of thing affected us much as if we had strayed into an opera-bouffe rehearsal (and the Halifax houses helped out the illusion, for they look like old scenery); but after a while we grew accustomed to all this scarlet and gold, and soon did not even turn our heads when we passed a pompous sergeant with his brilliant chevrons and purple sash.

"Do you know," said Thatcher, as the conversation fell back to the topic uppermost, after all, in our minds, "I think it is time we began taking some precautions. Here we are off for an out-of-the-way and almost unheard-of place after treasure, accompanied by a French cook and by as tough a customer as you could find anywhere on Montmartre. Doesn't such a combination appeal to you as unusual?"

"That last feature you mention of the situation is certainly sufficient to arouse suspicion in the mind of almost any one," I admitted.

"Exactly. That's why I think we ought, so far as possible, to keep dark our relations with Chiffard and the villain. That was my principal reason for wanting to put them off under a different roof."

"Yes; but, after all, I don't know that it makes much difference so long as we are going to sail directly from here in our own chartered schooner."

"Perhaps we shall not do that. I am

not by any means convinced of that's being the best plan.   Are you?"

" I don't know that I am, but we haven't
anything better in view just now.   Let's
go down to the docks and see what we
can find in the way of a schooner."

" We can spend our time to better advantage, I think," said Thatcher. " While
you were pigeon-holing the crew and the
cook, I was talking to a number of Nova
Scotian idiots around the hotel.   I never
struck a town where the average of information was so low; nevertheless, I managed to worm out something.   I posed
as a 'journalist'—bad cess to the word!—
on my way up to St. Pierre to 'write up'
the place for a syndicate, and—would you
believe it?—the first three men I braced
did not know there were any such islands
on the face of the sea.   Finally, however, I
found a fellow in the bar who told me that
Madden & Maddigan are the agents for
a steamship which boasts the name *La*

Patrie, that runs up to the Miquelon Islands every two weeks. Well, sir, I was so tickled at getting on some kind of a trail that I blew that fellow off to three Scotch whiskeys in about as many minutes, and you never saw so astonished a Nova Scotian in your life. So I want to look up Madden & Maddigan, and if the *crétin* who directed me knew what he was talking about, we ought to be somewhere near their shop now."

But the said *crétin*, like the majority of his race whom it was our fortune to meet in Halifax, had put us on the wrong scent, and, after walking around in a circle for some time, we ended up by chartering a conveyance, in which we rode for half an hour before the driver found any one who knew enough to tell him where Madden & Maddigan's was. At the end of that time we wandered into a narrow, roughly paved street, and drew up before a clean-looking stone building of very modest appearance, and over the low doorway hung the anchored sign of Madden & Maddigan.

"Now, mind you," said Thatcher, as he jumped out of the rickety *calèche*, "we are tourists—you and I, two of us only; you artist, I writer—and we want to go to St. Pierre. Let me do the talking, and be sure you back me up in all I say."

Before I could expostulate, he had pushed open the glass door of the low-ceilinged shipping-office and was leaning expectantly upon the polished counter. A clerk crawled out from behind a desk as we entered and stared at us with the imbecilic expression we were rapidly becoming accustomed to — an expression which Thatcher characterized as " the codfish face." When we told him we wanted to find out about transportation to St. Pierre, a momentary gleam of intelligence seemed to appear in his eyes, as if at some remote period he had heard the name of the place; and then he relapsed codfishy and said *La Patrie* sailed in a few days, but would not go to St. Pierre this trip. We attacked him from all points of the compass, and tried to confound his crass ignorance of his own business, hoping the man might unwittingly deliver himself of some useful fact; but all in vain. Then we asked if, perhaps, a member of the firm were in. Yes, Colonel Madden was in.

"Thank Heaven for that!" muttered Thatcher.

We were invited into a rear office, where we met a tall, loosely-built, military-looking man with a fine face, sunburned all over, except for a scallop over his right eye, where his little pill-box artilleryman's cap had protected a circle some three inches in diameter from the effects of sun exposure during a week in camp. To our unspeakable delight, Colonel Madden could tell us just what we wanted to know—and he did, too. We found we could go by steamship more or less directly to our destination, or we could go by rail as far as Sydney, at the extremity of Cape Breton, and thence take the same steamer to St. Pierre. He informed us thoroughly concerning prices and time, and even of the manners and customs of the folk we were going to. The one point he could not make clear—and that to himself—was why we should ever want to go to Miquelon. Thatcher attempted to satisfy his curiosity on that point, but even his glowing fiction and wild rhetoric failed to convince or enlighten the good Colonel, and he doubtless looks upon us to this day as harmless lunatics. Nevertheless, he offered to do everything he could for us if we should choose to go on his ship, and he convinced us of his goodwill by taking us into his club.

Over our pipes, after supper, we discussed our plans more comprehensively

in the light of the important information obtained from Colonel Madden. We
came to the conclusion, after very short
consideration, that such a quartet as we
were would possibly cause some comment if we were known to be travelling
together, and we soon agreed that it
would be far better if Chiffard and Carquemort could make their way independently to St. Pierre, and meet us on the
islands. The trouble would be in per-
suading the Frenchmen of this. We
both felt that Carquemort was already
becoming restless at the way in which
we were conducting the expedition, dis-
regarding him entirely and proceeding
along the line of our best judgment. He
had not complained, to be sure; but for
the past few days—in fact, from the hour
we left New York—the man had been silent and morose. Chiffard, who was most
with him, had commented to us upon it;
and we had also overheard him say to

Carquemort one night that he would rather travel around the world with a mangy dog than go a day's journey with such a sullen beast as he. And Carquemort had made no reply; so we held the opinion that he was in drink—but whence he got the money to pay for his sullenness we could not guess.

After a protracted session, we concluded that our best plan, and the swiftest, would be for the four of us to go by rail to North Sydney, in Cape Breton. Between St. Pierre and this place there is a lively trade in coal and kindling-wood, and a powerful traffic in smuggling. We believed we could hire a schooner for a song at Sydney, a schooner that had run in the smuggling line, if possible, for her skipper would be just the kind of a man we needed for the business in hand. And so it was that our stay in Halifax was cut shorter than we had anticipated; and we left on the railroad early in the morning of the second day after we had fastened upon our determination.

The time intervening we spent in the purchase of spades and picks, hammers and chisels, a quantity of heavy canvas sacks, and several pounds of blasting powder and dynamite. This we had some trouble in securing; in fact, we feared we must do without. But Carquemort, when we had failed, took our money and promised to secure the explosives. A villain himself, he must have dealt with his kind; for, an hour later, he returned with the goods, and the price we paid was double the market rate. Whether it was Carquemort who profited by this transaction, it is difficult to say; but from what Chiffard reported the next morning, Carquemort was far from sober that night, and I much fear he led the cook beyond temptation, for both men were sorry passengers on the shuffling, colonial train that beautiful July day.

CHAPTER VIII

A PLAN OF OPERATIONS

THE little town of North Sydney nestles in the knee of a deep bay on the northeastern coast of Cape Breton, and straggles along the shore in a single, narrow, ill-kept street that lifts itself up out of the coal-mines near the hollow of the harbor and stretches off aimlessly to the northward until it loses itself in a waste of rocks and dwarf pine. Everything about the place is grimy with coal, the air is heavy and soggy with fog, and all nature seems dull and gray. The chill sea-water laps mournfully against the sides of the coaling craft that lie along the shaky, moss-grown docks, and the rattling of pulleys, the creaking of derrick-booms, the groaning of steam winches, with every now and then the hoarse roar of a load of coal dumped from a trestle, make the only sounds that cut into the bleak and melancholy stillness of the place.

It was night when we came to Sydney —black, misty night, and the trees dripped in the darkness. By the grace of a small native with a lantern, we felt our way slowly and with an ungovernable sense of apprehension through the stubble fields that separate the terminus of the railroad from the inhabited quarter of the town. Thatcher carried the explosives, which he was reluctant to intrust even to my care, and Carquemort, cursing, stumbled along in the murk behind, while Chiffard clung to the circle of the lantern's rays, ever and again looking back over his shoulder towards Thatcher and his death-dealing burden. The dim glare of the swinging lantern sent our shadows

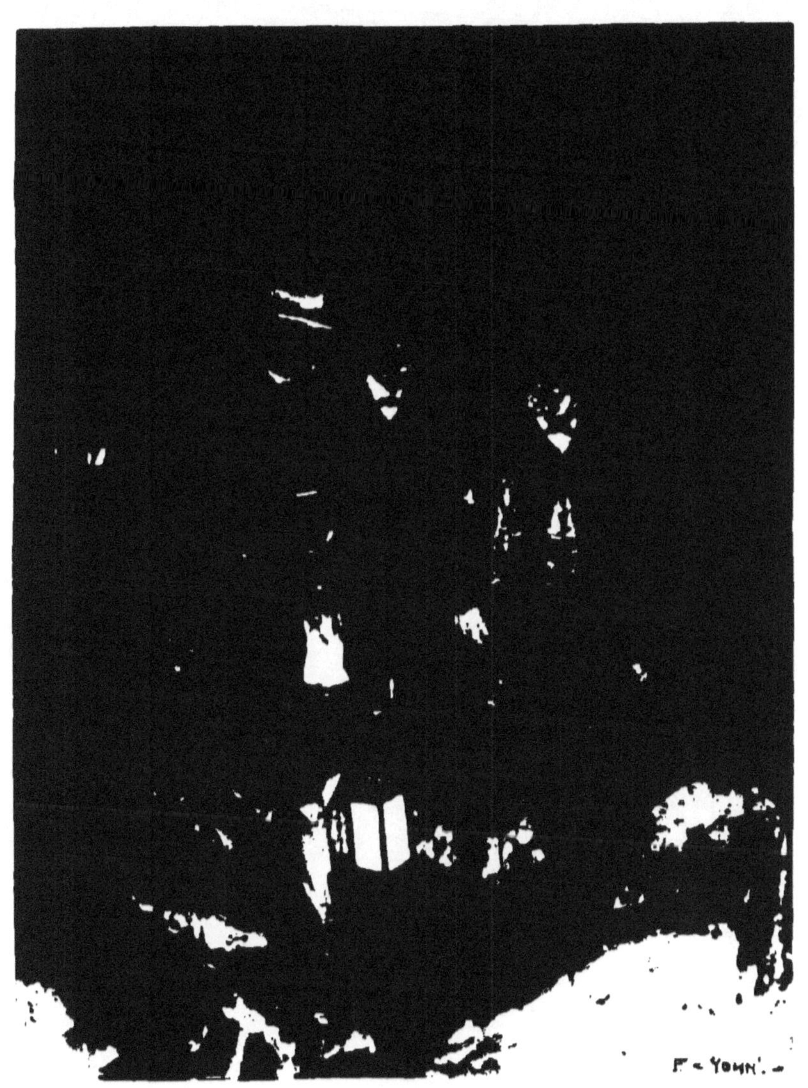

A SMALL BOY GUIDED US THROUGH THE DARKNESS

stalking like bodiless giants through the last patch of woods, and finally we turned into the silent street. Here there was scarce more light than in the by-ways, a faint beam falling across the ruts here and there from under the drawn curtain of some sailors' shore-side tavern.

The boy led us to a dingy, unventilated inn, that backs up on a dock and boasts the proud name "Hôtel des Ambassadeurs." The proprietor welcomed us in a sleepy, unintelligent, Nova Scotian fashion, but he earned our good-will at once by defying the Scott Act without further ceremony. Our walk through the fog-laden atmosphere had chilled us to the marrow — and, in addition, his whiskey was excellent. We marvelled at its quality and commented upon it; but our host was not vainglorious. Later we understood why, and wondered we had not suspected the reason from the first.

The proprietor's name was Holtz, or at

least so he was generally called by his neighbors, but he assured us over the second bottle that his full name was Sammelholtz. He seemed to us a surly fellow at the start, but developed qualities as the bowl's tide ebbed. In spite of his increased geniality and openness, however, we never quite made him out. He looked like a Scotchman, he had the Gaelic, he spoke English with a non-Scotch accent, he had a German name, and he claimed to be French—backing this by bawling a *patois* at Carquemort and Chiffard. But, poor devil! no wonder he had lost his identity, living, as he had for years, in that bleak northern hole where winter is long and summer but a mockery, and life altogether a dull, beast-like existence at best.

Beyond ourselves there seemed to be no guests at the Hôtel des Ambassadeurs. Consequently we had the full choice of apartments, and, the rates being cheap,

Thatcher and I each took a room, and we packed off our Frenchmen to a chamber within call, at the end of the narrow passageway. So constantly were we now subject to the spell of the feverish excitement of our enterprise that sleep sat lightly upon our eyes, and it had almost become a necessity for us to puff at our pipes for an hour or more each night, and talk, talk, talk—rehearsing the same hopes and reviewing the same fears, the whole to a pepper - and - salt flavoring of international profanity by Thatcher—before we could compose ourselves for a much-needed repose.

"There is one good thing about that blackguard Carquemort," said Thatcher, as we conversed; " he does not talk about our private affairs, no matter how drunk he may be."

"He's got sense enough for that," I said. " He would never have spoken to us in Chiffard's if he had not been driven to it by the need of financial aid. Do you think we made a mistake in letting Holtz — or Sammelholtz, or whatever his name is — know we were all four together?"

" I hardly think so," answered Thatcher. " I rather suspect Holtz is a bit deep himself. He never paid duty on that whiskey, or he could not sell it at the price he does, or even keep it—in such a hole as this. I have an idea we've stumbled over the right man in him. He may prove of considerable service to us."

" I hope he may. We might enlist his services by giving him the impression that we are up to some sort of a smuggling scheme — which in reality we are. He is a close-mouthed customer apparently. There is no harm in sounding him."

" None whatever. He may be just the man to fit out our expedition, schooner and all. The fellows who sailed that whiskey into this port ought to be available to navigate a little bullion and coin down to Boston or New York."

"So you still consider it advisable to get our schooner here and invade St. Pierre," I said, "rather than to learn first if we have any cargo, and hire the transport in the islands afterwards?"

"By all means. The chances are we should have trouble getting a boat up there. It's a very small place, you know, and there's a governor, with a garrison, and paternal government, and all that sort of thing; and French law claims half of treasure-trove — and if we 'trove' any, you can bet your boots we are not dividing with any government! We are putting the stuff aboard ship and skipping for home as tight as the merry winds will blow us!" and Thatcher slapped his knee loudly by way of emphasis. "I don't relish the idea, however, of sailing up to those islands in a foul-smelling tub, and I never have taken much to that part of the programme since it was first suggested."

" I don't relish it myself," I admitted. " But I think we ought to do what is for the best."

" So do I, of course, but I doubt if it is necessary for us to coop ourselves up in any schooner just yet. We can just as well send Chiffard and Carquemort off on the boat and ourselves seek St. Pierre by steamer."

Thatcher was warming to his argument. " Any schooner we get must have some sort of excuse for putting into the port of St. Pierre. Coal is the best subterfuge we can adopt in these parts. The schooner makes St. Pierre with her coal and kindling and the skipper gives out that he wants to pick up a cheap cargo of cod. In the mean time you and I, artist and writer again, take the good *La Patrie*, which touches here next

Wednesday—you heard Holtz say so to-night—and land comfortably in St. Pierre. We are going to make an indefinite stay in the colony; we take up our lodgings in some quiet neighborhood where we can go in and out at all hours; we hang around the docks and scrape acquaintance with the fishermen — looking for 'local color,' you know.   In this way we make the acquaintance of Chiffard and Carque-mort and of the other thugs we shall by that time have in our employ, and we at once set about surveying that direct line from the cross on the Ile aux Chiens to the mast.   See?"

" All that sounds very well," I said, "but how about putting it through ?"

" We've put everything through, so far, have not we?"

I was forced to admit that we had.

" Very well," he continued, "if you approve of this now I'll see that it's put through if I have to knock the logic of it into Carquemort with my two fists. What do you say?"

"Amen!" I shouted.

"That settles it, then," said Thatcher, jumping to his feet. "Take one more nip of Holtz's best, and get to your dreams. It is three o'clock."

CHAPTER IX

EXPLANATIONS AND NEGOTIATIONS

THE following day broke clear and fresh, and a brisk wind from the east carried the odor of the deep sea in at our windows. We looked forth into the glad morning and saw the sunlight dancing on the quivering waters of the bay like the visions of gold that ceaselessly twinkled in our own minds. Even the scraggy shores back of South Sydney, opposite, looked a little less bleak and arid, and here and there a tuft of verdure forced itself up above the gray monotone of the sky-line. Distance lent beauty to the moving fishing craft in the harbor, and the sight of sails inspired us to renewed activity.

We found our Frenchmen below and

satiate, and when ourselves had breakfasted the four of us gathered in one of
the upper rooms and opened a conference
behind bolted doors.   Thatcher unfolded
in detail the plan he had roughly outlined
to me the night before, and Chiffard, as
the more intelligent of our two associ-
ates, pronounced at once in favor of it.
So emphatic was his approval that his
fist fairly cracked the table-top, and the
old petard spirit rolled out in cataractic
French.   But Carquemort was silent and
shifted about uneasily in his chair.

" I don't like this separating business,"
he said, finally. " We are all four to
share equally in the benefits of the treasure, and it seems to me all four ought to
share in the work."

" We are, none of us, trying to shirk
any work, Carquemort," I returned, sharply. " We are trying to arrange matters
so that the French authorities will not
interfere with us."

" They won't interfere with us," he retorted, sullenly.

" Do you mean to tell me that if we four, with perhaps a couple of men additional in the crew, arrive in the harbor of St. Pierre on a coaling schooner without any apparent object in view, with no cargo and in search of none, the authorities would not at once be suspicious of such actions and put a watch on us?"

" By gad!" cried Thatcher, " they never would pick us for a combination to travel for pleasure, especially in the tub we'll be able to get here. They'd take us for smugglers—you can bet your share on that!—and the first thing you'd know they'd have us all in the jug!"

Carquemort shrugged his shoulders.

" If your head is too thick to understand this," I continued, " you'll have to take our word for it—that's all. We've got to arrange things so that we can make our surveys and searches without arousing any one's suspicions, and the only way to do that is to adopt Thatcher's plan, or something like it. Can you suggest anything better?"

"Yes!" snorted Chiffard, "*sacrebleu*, can you suggest anything better?—*fichu chameau, vas!*"

Carquemort scowled, but gave no direct reply. Instead, he put another question:

"If we find the gold, then what?"

"If we find the gold, we pack it aboard the schooner."

"All of it?"

"All of it, of course. Do you suppose we're going to leave part of it behind?"

"What I want to know is whether *all* the gold comes back on the schooner, or if part of it goes back on the steamship. If it does not all go on the schooner, I—"

"You confounded blockhead!" interrupted Thatcher, with an enforcement of brutal oaths (for he had found that such methods worked best with the man), "how the deuce could we ship gold through the regular channels without the fact becoming known? What do you imagine we should want to take a schooner over there for if we could conceive of any other way of getting the treasure away from the islands secretly?"

This argument, and the tone of its delivery, appeared to have some influence with Carquemort, for he looked up and asked:

"And you two Americans?"

"What about us?"

"How do you come back?"

"You can bet your sweet life we come back with the gold!" I shouted. And so great was my vehemence that the other three laughed outright, which was a fortunate thing, for this unexpected hilarity helped considerably to clear the conversational atmosphere.

It was curious to consider how we had come to look upon the existence of the treasure as a certainty. The serious doubts of reasonable and right-minded men which we had formerly held concerning the genuineness of the chart had now vanished altogether, and we no longer even harbored any fears lest other hunters or chance diggers might have taken the gold from its hiding-place years ago. The single remaining obstacle which we recognized in our speculations and discussions were the difficulties we must encounter in locating the *cachette*. That done, we looked upon the rest as merely a matter of patience and muscle — or dynamite—and the conjectures as to our separate dividends fluctuated between the thousands and the millions; for, as Chiffard said, it was just as easy to add an extra zero or two before the treasure was unearthed, since this could not in any way affect the eventual result, and it certainly did give flavor to our constant diet of boiled and fried cod. Chiffard, in his own culinary way, was more or less of a philosopher.

So it was that we eventually brought Carquemort to look upon the proposed separation as a part of the comedy we must act, and he agreed to take his role with the rest of us, the only stipulations being that he have a voice in the selection of the schooner and the crew, and that if gold were found we all sail away from the islands together. We could not quite understand his persistent desire to have us on board the treasure - laden schooner, but we did not bother much about it, because we had never even remotely contemplated the idea of intrusting the fruits of our quest, might they be ever so small, to such a rascal as Carquemort.

"If we find but a thousand dollars," observed Thatcher, "I shall not only convoy it to New York myself, but. I mean to sit upon it by day and sleep upon it by night, until I get a deposit-slip for it from the receiving-teller of my bank."

Having converted the men to our own views, we went down-stairs and sought out Holtz, whom we found in the little back room where he had entertained us on our arrival the night before. Thatcher pulled his hat over his eyes and looked as mysterious as he could, and glanced about the room as if he feared there might be agents of the secret police concealed somewhere, and then addressed our host in what I should have appreciated as a very melodramatic manner if I had not been in such a peculiar mental condition consequent upon this whole treasure-hunting business. But I saw nothing comical in the situation then. Now, as I look back upon it, I can enjoy it all to its full extent, and the subsequent tragedies do not in the least, so far as I am concerned, cast gloom over the farce-comedies that went before.

"You have some acquaintance among the watermen of this port?" Thatcher began.

Holtz nodded his head non-committally.

"Well, we are looking for a schooner that we can get to take us over to St. Pierre, and wait for us until we get ready to come away, and either sail us back to Halifax or to some port in the States."

"Why don't you go to St. Pierre on *La Patrie?*" asked Holtz.

"Well," drawled Thatcher, as he blew a great cloud of smoke towards the ceiling and then looked steadily at the hotel proprietor, " I am told that St. Pierre is a most interesting place, and we may find some things up there that we should like to bring back; and possibly it might not be just convenient for us to ship them on *La Patrie*—do you see? We don't want to go through a lot of formalities, you know."

" O-o-o-h !" exclaimed Holtz, in a very low, long sort of whistle; " I understand." And he looked long and searchingly at both of us. " I wondered why you gentlemen came with those two "—and he jerked his head to one side, as indicating Chiffard and Carquemort. " They are seamen ?"

" Both," replied Thatcher. " We want two more, I guess—a master and an A. B. The skipper must be a man with a level head, and no mouth, no eyes, no ears, no memory !"

" Perhaps we can do something," said Holtz, musingly. " I know a man who forgets very quick," and he chuckled at his own sally. Then he rose from his seat and stepped to a window facing the bay and called to a boy, who sat swinging his legs on the end of the dock, to run down and fetch Captain McLeod, if he was at home.

" McLeod is about the man you want,

I guess," he said, as he sat down again. " He knows those Newfoundland waters as he knows his pocket. And," he added, impressively, " there's nobody knows anything about Captain John McLeod's business, because Captain John McLeod don't advertise in the newspapers." And here Holtz chuckled again and looked from one to the other of us to note the effect of his wit.

I never should have picked out Holtz for a man imbued with delicacy and tact, and the spirit which prompted him to act as he presently did may have been far from either of these qualities. But whatever it was, when, fifteen or twenty minutes later, a short, stocky, bearded seaman came stumping into the hotel, Holtz arose, and, having shaken hands with his friend, introduced him to us, and then walked forthwith out of the room, closing the door behind him, without saying a word or offering any explanation whatever to the sea-captain. Possibly that is the way business of this nature is transacted in Sydney and similar places, for the new-comer seemed to take it all as a matter of course. As for ourselves, we were just as well pleased to have as few cooks to our broth as were absolutely necessary.

So we shook hands all around, and poured a full glass for the captain, who drew a chair up to the table and crossed his short legs and folded his hard, knotted hands, and sat calmly waiting for one of us to speak, showing no more embarrassment than if he had known us all his life. And this is odd for a seafaring man.

CHAPTER X

THE CAPTAIN OF THE *MERRY MADGE*

CAPTAIN McLEOD was a Cape Bretonese Scot, and I judge his years were fifty. He came originally from a village of the Bras d'Or, but for the past twenty-five years or more he had lived in and out of Sydney, mostly on sea. I was not greatly taken with his countenance, but I presume it is scarcely fair to look for soft-voiced, mild-mannered men in the trade he followed. His hair was close cropped on a bullet head, and his pale, sea-colored eyes moved slowly but ceaselessly from one side of the room to the other, or from the ceiling to the floor. He had a scar down his right cheek which fell across the corner of his mouth and gave a peculiar and ghastly expression to his face when he smiled — which was not often, thank Heaven. He was shaven along the upper lip and to a point just below the ears, but his chin and throat bristled with a short, stubby beard that resembled horse-hair.

Thatcher opened the proceedings without any diplomatic parleying and went directly to the point, stating our case almost in the first sentence—an audacious proceeding which undoubtedly bore weight with the sailorman.

" Captain," he said, " we want to go up to St. Pierre Miquelon, on a little matter of business and pleasure combined. We are looking for a schooner, snug and sea-worthy, and a skipper who knows those waters. We may wish to remain up there two weeks—we may find ourselves compelled to stay two months."

McLeod grunted and glanced up quickly, first at one of us and then at the other.

" I have a little eighty-ton schooner anchored off the point down here," he said, " and as soon as I can put in enough kindling-wood and coal, I'm going up to the French islands myself. I usually take the *Merry Madge* over there two or three times a year; but I never carried any passengers," and McLeod again looked up quizzically. Thatcher seemed to understand.

" There are four of us," he said. " Two are to go on the schooner, two will go on *La Patrie*." And then he added, slowly and impressively, placing the tip of his extended forefinger upon the captain's knee: " But from the time the schooner we hire leaves her mooring here until she lands us again at any port we may designate between St. John's and Philadelphia, *we* control her absolutely — do you understand? — *absolutely*. We take all risks, too — and we're willing to pay what's right."

"Ah!" exclaimed McLeod, thoughtfully. "Of course, it's none of my business what you gentlemen are going up there for; and I'd just as lief not know anything about it. I ain't going to ask any questions. I'll just sail the *Merry Madge* as you say; and while I'm under contract to you, I'll do as you wish, bar running her on the rocks."

"That's understood, then. We're boss, and what we say goes."

"What you say goes," assented McLeod. "Where are the others?"

"I'll call them," said I, rising.

"No; hold up a bit," interposed Thatcher, and, turning to the captain, "What's your price?"

McLeod did not hesitate a second: "Three hundred dollars, cash down in the Dominion Bank here, before we start."

"And for how long does that give us control of the schooner?"

"You said you wanted her about two months. If you require her a month longer we can come to an understanding later, easy enough. This figure includes my services, but you pay the crew."

" How many men do you want in the forecastle ?"

" Two can work her; three would do better."

" We'll give you a seaman and a cook —the two men with us; you get the others."

" My son, for one," said the captain; " and there's always plenty of hands hanging around the coal docks."

" Very well; that 'll make four besides yourself, and the cook can stand his watch with the rest. Our fellows are both French."

" That's all right," grinned McLeod; " I can talk to the beasts; I've had Canucks on the *Merry Madge* before this," and he ripped out a French oath as a

sort of confirmation of his linguistic ca-
pabilities.

" You'll do," laughed Thatcher; " now
let's look at the boat."

We picked up Chiffard and Carquemort at the door; the latter looking somewhat sour, for I guess he had expected to
be called in with McLeod. But he said
nothing, and we set off down the street,
Thatcher and the captain walking on
ahead, with Carquemort dogging their
heels, while Chiffard and I followed leisurely behind.

The *Merry Madge* was swinging to a
barrel buoy about ten cable-lengths from
shore, just beyond a rocky little point
where the town begins to lose itself in
the scrub pine wilderness half a mile or
so beyond the Hôtel des Ambassadeurs.
She was not, by any means, a beautiful
craft to look upon, being rather more
square - prowed than what you see in
Gloucester, but McLeod explained as we

neared her that she was built to crunch through the ice eight months of the year. She sat low in the water, and her dirty, coal-soiled sails swung half-hoist, bleaching in the sunlight.

"Lend a hand there, Crackmug!" shouted the captain to our friend, Carquemort, as we reached the pebbly shore. "Chuck those oars into that dory, and slide her down lively, now! And see here, you jab sea cook"—to Chiffard—"limber up now, limber up! Don't you see the painter's going foul of that stake there? '*Cré mille millions de pipes !*"

Carquemort was somewhat surprised at these unexpected commands, but (from habit, doubtless) he did not hesitate to obey; he grabbed one side of the heavy dory that lay high and dry on the beach, while the captain laid hold of the other gunwale, and between the two of them they launched her easily; while Chiffard, who had been playing the *grand seigneur* for over a week, stood like a stone image and glared at McLeod as if he had been insulted; and I sprang to catch the trailing painter just in time to keep the dory from sliding adrift.

Thatcher smiled. " You're a sailor now, Chiffard," he said; "steward and cook of the *Merry Madge*, or will be if we find her ship-shape and suitable. You've got to remember you're not in New York now, and that McLeod's captain of his boat and your superior. You know what that means; you've got sense. You have not dug up any gold yet, you know."

Chiffard laughed and nodded, and cursed in an undertone; but he knew what was expected of him and what he might expect, and his early experience at sea stood him in good stead.

" I'll do what's right," he said, "but I wish to Heaven it was all over. To think of *père* Chiffard ' aye, aye '-ing to a crab like that !"

In the mean time Carquemort and the captain had brought the dory alongside of a dilapidated float near by, and we quickly clambered in.

"Tumble into the bow there, *chef!*" shouted McLeod, "and play ballast for the gentlemen in the stern-sheets. Fall away!" He and Carquemort were at the oars, and it did me good to see the latter, for the first time since I had known him, doing some work.

We found the captain's son, Glen, swabbing down decks, and he was powerfully surprised to see the company his father brought over the rail with him. He was a likely looking lad for a Cape Bretonese, some two-and-twenty years of age, I guess, built square from top to toe, but apparently not the mental equal of his ancestor.

As soon as Chiffard set foot on the schooner's deck he recovered his usual good-humor, and drew in great lungfuls of the salt air that rushed over the bow and fell out of the drying sails. "*Ah, sacristi, que ça sent bon !*" he exclaimed; and he went stomping up forward to scrape acquaintance with young McLeod.

"We shall not want you," said Thatcher, turning to Carquemort, who hung near by. "We're going below to talk business with the captain, and until we return you can look over the schooner and see if she fills the bill." Then, as we crawled down the companion-way into the cabin, Thatcher said to the captain: "You want to treat our two men white, if you can. They're in a sort of partnership with us on this deal;" and he added: "I don't mean by that you're to take any nonsense."

"You bet I won't," returned McLeod. "The men on this schooner do what I tell 'em, and they do it well and P. D. Q.! But I guess I know what you mean, and I'll hold it in mind. But, mind you, this trip ain't a picnic for the hands. Those fellows ain't passengers."

"Not a bit of it," said I. "They're here to work, but don't drive 'em."

"If they do their work properly they'll find Captain John McLeod is *their* man." And the old sea-dog slowly closed one eye in a self-appreciative and confident wink.

CHAPTER XI

A CONTRACT

THE cabin of the *Merry Madge* was not roomy, nor particularly clean ; neither was its atmosphere so pure and bracing as that which had delighted Chiffard on deck, but no doubt the arrangements were as good as could be expected aboard an eighty-ton coaling schooner, and, on the whole, things might have been a great deal worse. There were two so-called state-rooms, one on either side of the companion-way, the starboard compartment being the captain's room. "Sometimes I let Glen sleep in the other," explained McLeod, "but mostly he bunks for'ard. It's good for him." A narrow table ran down the centre of the cabin under the skylight, and along the sides were set a couple of broad lockers, cushioned on top so that they might, if necessary, be used for bunks. "One of you passengers 'll have to take up there, I guess," laughed the captain. "You can toss for the other room." Then he stepped over to a cupboard and brought down a brown bottle and some glasses. "I guess you can't beat this Madeira, even in New York," he said. "Captain McDavitt brought it over to me from Cadiz; that's his barkentine tied up to the wharf back of the hotel," he added; "she trades in salt."

"This is pretty good salt," I said, as I drank half a glassful of the wine. I had never tasted better.

"Yes," answered McLeod. "There's money in salt, if you know what kind to buy," and he chuckled softly as he held his glass up to the light.

Thereupon we turned to a discussion of the business in hand. McLeod said there were some twenty tons of coal in the hold already, and that he had intended putting in more during the week; but he was willing, if we could advance a part of the contract price, to put down to the coal-trestles on Monday and take on another twenty tons. Then he thought he could get kindling-wood from a village a couple of miles inland the next day, and be ready to put to sea Wednesday on the early tide. The captain was more anxious about the kindling than the coal. "There isn't a tree on those islands," he explained, "and Johnny Crapaud has to buy all his firewood from us or the Newfoundlanders. Those Burin fellows run over in dories from the French shore, but they can't carry any such load as I'll put in if I have luck." He then wanted to know how much cargo space we wanted for the return trip, but, to his credit, he beat the devil around the stump a long while before he put the question.

IN THE CABIN OF THE *MERRY MADGE*

"That's what we can't tell," I answered. "We really don't know ourselves, captain; but I reckon the cabin will hold all we'll bring off!"

"The cabin?" exclaimed McLeod, in surprise.

"The cabin," I repeated; "but we'll see."

"Oh," said McLeod, good-naturedly, "any one might think you were going after diamonds! But I was not asking out of curiosity," he continued. "I want to know if I'll have room to take on a load of cod."

"You are going to St. Pierre," said Thatcher, "to *sell* coal and *buy* cod, Mr. McLeod. Do you understand that? That's what you are going there for."

"I guess I see that," said the captain.

"And you're in no hurry for your cod —do you see? You are willing to wait for the price to go down."

"Surely," nodded McLeod. "I'll find

out who's in port, and I'll be waiting to buy my fish from the fellow that's on the banks."

" That's the idea," said Thatcher; and then he roughly outlined a contract in pencil, covering all these points, and we agreed to sign Monday after the money had been deposited in the Dominion Bank. Take it all in all, we felt satisfied with our man—and the one thing above all others that compelled our admiration was his capacity for minding his own business.

When we got back to our quarters at the Hotel des Ambassadeurs, Carque- mort, very much to our surprise, express- ed himself as perfectly satisfied with the schooner *Merry Madge;* and when, after supper, we read off Thatcher's outline of the contract, both men approved, and said they would do their share towards working the schooner up to the islands. The only objection Carquemort made was to the charter price; but that objection was not very vigorous since the money did not come out of his pocket. So delighted was I at the progress we had made and at Carquemort's decency and demeanor, that I was fool enough to give him a two-dollar bill, bidding him drink to our good luck and to his new berth, which he did faithfully, and the next day he was of no use—a condition which we ultimately envied him, for a Sunday in Sydney, Cape Breton, is a dreadful and interminable experience. But, like all things, it came to an end, and the next two days saw us most diversely occupied.

Everything progressed satisfactorily, and by Tuesday evening McLeod had his coal and kindling-wood snugly stowed away in the hold of the *Merry Madge*, and everything was in readiness for the schooner to put to sea early the following morning.

The fourth hand for the crew had been

shipped—and, strange to say, upon Carquemort's recommendation. Carquemort had discovered him Saturday night in some den of the town, and the two had drunk together, and he would have us believe he had known the fellow before; but we all doubted this part of the story. The man was a Finn, by name Semsen—tall, lean, sunken-eyed, but a deep-sea sailor through and through, and he satisfied McLeod the moment he clapped eyes upon him. This being the case, we were willing to ship him; and we were further urged to this course that it might seem to Carquemort as if he were a factor in our counsels. For this bit of sentiment we paid dearly in the end, as all must who allow sentiment to interfere with business.

We were up with the larks on Wednesday and walked down to the point. McLeod rowed in from the *Merry Madge* for a few last words and then pulled back;

and Thatcher and I stood upon the shore and listened to the creaking of the blocks and the bawling of orders until the cable was slipped from the mooring, and the breeze bent the little collier to a graceful angle, and the water bubbled in her wake as she moved slowly out of the bay. We realized now, more fully than we had at any time before, that we were fairly launched upon our enterprise, and we were scarcely able to control the powerful emotions that rose within us. We stood in silence, and never turned our eyes from the boat until at last she fell off behind the low headland and disappeared. Then we turned slowly away.

CHAPTER XII

A VOYAGE OVER-SEAS

LONG, narrow, high-prowed *La Patrie*, with the tricolor of France floating lazily from the taffrail, put into Sydney a couple of hours later, having come up through the Golden Lakes from Baddeck. She groaned and snorted and whistled, and made much ado, after the Gallic fashion; and her deck-racing, wildly gesticulating officers almost had nervous prostration over getting her into dock; all of which afforded much amusement to the Sydney wharf-loungers, who laughed uproariously and cast back ribald taunts in answer to the polysyllabic oaths belched into the air by the motley French crew.

"The blooming maniacs!" muttered

Holtz; "they give us this bloody show every two weeks," and he turned away in disgust.

There was, in truth, a good deal of the spectacular about the management of this good ship, as Holtz had justly said—that is, it was spectacular from an Anglo-Saxon point of view, but doubtless, to the Frenchmen, very serious business.

The afternoon was spent in coaling, and at nine o'clock in the evening, after the mail-train from civilization had arrived, there was bustle and commotion, and a prodigious sound of voices on the deck. Then, after some delay, a vociferous exhortation from the bridge was sent rattling down the speaking-tube to the engineer asking why in the name of all the thousand thunders, and such other of the elements as are invoked by the French, he did not start his machines. To which the engineer replied in muffled tones, from the bowels of the ship, that he was no mind-reader, and that no signal had yet been given, and would any one believe, *par example*, that a ship-captain could be such an infernal idiot as not to know enough to pull the signal-bell when he was ready to start? Whereupon ensued a long-distance quarrel full of picturesque verbiage and marine simile, which ended by the captain calling upon the man at the wheel as witness that he had pulled the cord. The quartermaster was compelled to side with the engineer, and assured the captain that he must have overlooked the little formality; thereupon a stream of apology was sent gurgling downward through the speaking-trumpet, and the engineer's acceptance soon came bubbling upward, and, after a pleasant exchange of courtesies and jests, the machinery-man asked if the captain was ready to start now, and the captain replied that he was if the engineer was; and so, presently, the engines began to wheeze and strain and the episode was closed, and the departure had, after all, been delayed not more than fifteen minutes, which is insignificant when you consider how much more important it is that the officers of a ship should thoroughly understand one another.

Thus it is plain that life upon the good ship *La Patrie* was void of that excessive formality which breeds stiffness and, perhaps, discomfort — two conditions which, at sea, of all places, are repugnant to the Latin temperament.

We found a strange and mixed company on board: three priests from Antigonish bound for St. Johns; an American merchant of St. Pierre, genial and florid, and full of quaint oaths and strange hyperbole, and half a score of good, plain St. Pierrese, returning from their vacations. Among the latter was a pleasant and garrulous old gentleman, a great-grandfather, who, we were told, was the "oldest inhabitant."

"Just our man," said Thatcher; and the next morning, as the ship rolled easily over the glassy sea, we made M. de Manclay's acquaintance. He was a friendly soul, superlatively communicative and overflowing with anecdote. When we told him we were going to the islands for the pure pleasure of sojourning a few weeks among its people, the good old gentleman expanded as a morning-glory opens to the rising sun, and the thrilling history of France's only remaining possession in North America fell from his lips in an absorbing and enthusiastic narrative. He told us of himself and of what he had seen and done in the long years that had stretched away to the birth of the century through the perspective of his life, and he revelled in the romance of warfare and the sea.

"*Croiriez-vous bien, messieurs*," he continued, dramatically, "that I likewise saw some of the terrors of your own civil war?

I went down to Baltimore to buy a schooner for my fishing enterprises. I took my men with me, and I sailed her back to St. Pierre myself. Off Cape Ann we saw a couple of Confederate privateers (*des corsaires du Sud*, he called them) overhaul and capture a dozen fishing-smacks from Gloucester, and they lashed them together and set them on fire. It was evening, and we saw the glare and smoke even after the conflagration had sunk below the horizon to the south of us. *Ah, la guerre, mes jeunes amis, c'est terrible!*"

And so the morning hours wore away, and incidentally we picked up a vast amount of information which must be useful to us in our impending endeavors.

Along towards noon the fog fell and shut us in upon the heaving bosom of an unrippled sea. The ship bowed rhythmically to the ground-swell, and only the measured thump, thump, thump of the propeller, deep astern, broke the absolute silence of our surroundings. Occasionally the man at the wheel bethought himself of the requirements of navigation, and pulled a hoarse blast from the fog-horn; but so long as he could even see a ship's length ahead of him he refrained from this exertion. Along about two o'clock there came evidences that we were nearing land. We began to catch sight of dories off in the mist, two fishermen in each, tending their cod lines. Occasionally the captain stopped the steamer and conversed with the dorymen over the rail, and the dorymen talked in an unintelligible patois and pointed hither and yon, and gave us our bearings. And thus *La Patrie* felt her way cautiously in towards the islands.

Then, all of a sudden, out of the absolute stillness of the cloud-banks there came a deep, long-drawn moan—the warning of a fog-horn, the big steam-whistle on Galantry Head, at the entrance of St.

Pierre harbor. It made a weird and ghastly noise, the note being so arranged that it trembled and vibrated like the hoarse bleating of some mammoth sheep. The sensation upon first hearing this fearsome sound, that seemed to come out of nowhere from the mist and darkness, was peculiar, and suggestive of uncanny things. This ghastly howl of distress bore over the silent water like the wail of some giant - child — some Frankenstein of the North that had become lost in the fog, and was crying out for help as it wandered alone over the ocean wilderness.

We could tell from the curving wake that the vessel was pointing in towards the sound. Soon there was a rift in the mist, and the thickest of the fog seemed to lift; and there, on the port bow, barely three ship's lengths from us, rose the bleak, rocky Galantry Head, with the slender light-house towering on its brow and the dreadful fog - horn bellowing amid the breakers at its base. The helm went hard down, and we swung into the channel for the harbor. This lies straight and narrow between the Head and a small island where a little white fishing village clusters about a church and a light-house, and so narrow is its course that our faces, as we leaned eagerly over the rail, were splashed by the spray that flew from the surf on the rocks.

" That," said M. de Manclay, pointing to the island, " is l'Ile aux Chiens."

What a magic name for us! How we leaned and craned our necks and stared at the little settlement, and tried to pierce the very fog-banks with our vision, searching for the " cross " that had so long delayed and puzzled us in the early stages of our adventure. But we could see no cross, and we thought best, for the present, to ask no questions. We mistrusted our own eagerness.

A little breeze had sprung up meanwhile from over Newfoundland way, and the heavy rolls of mist rose slowly and went scurrying off to leeward, leaving the fair little French town of St. Pierre all uncurtained before us. We exclaimed at the rude beauty of this sudden vision, and I felt, for one, that if even now our quest proved vain, the voyage to such a delightful spot was well worth the time and trouble we had expended upon it.

Picture to yourself a village of about three thousand souls nestled near the top of some noble Alpine mountain, far up above the timber line, where there are no trees, no bushes, no verdure of any kind—only bleak, bare, dun-colored rocks that tower a thousand feet or more above the slated roofs and the church steeples. Then let your imagination raise the sea up to the very edge of this Alpine village; dot the tortuous outer harbor with surf-smitten bowlders; place here and there a little white light-house clinging to one of these slippery pedestals, crowd the inner basin with hundreds of luggers, barks, and brown-sailed fishing schooners. Such is St. Pierre! It is a mountain town' in mid-Atlantic.

CHAPTER XIII

A BAD START

WE took up our lodgings in a quaint little house in a narrow lane of a street that sloped down towards the quays, and we slept peacefully that night in high mahogany bedsteads, under spreading, old-fashioned canopies. No sound disturbed our slumbers after the bold drummer had gone his rounds, rolling out curfew and beating the St. Pierrese to rest; and we were called again to the business of another day by the martial notes of the town-crier's bugle. St. Pierre rises to the clarion and retires to the scolding rumble of a sheepskin.

Our first move upon sallying forth was the purchase of a map of the islands;

our second, an excursion across the harbor to the Ile aux Chiens. As many dogs, upon so restricted an acreage, I never saw before; and their friendliness was surpassed only by the good-natured curiosity of the islanders. Rightly was the rock named Dog Island; but, as Thatcher noted, while we searched in vain for the cross mentioned on Carquemort's chart, "The cross seems rather to be in the breed of dogs than concretely erect upon the face of the cliff."

And, indeed, the comment was zoologically just. For, at a more or less remote period in the history of this colony some one must have imported a dachshund. That dachshund launched into a career of impetuous and reckless paternity, with the result that the influence of his breed is now plainly demonstrate in the forelegs of every cur in town. It must surely shock any dog-fancier to visit Miquelon's

Ile aux Chiens, for there he will encounter red Irish setters, and pointers,
and fox-terriers, with limbs only half as
long as they should be — the preambu-
lators knock-kneed and squatty. The
noble, pure-blooded Newfoundland that
we had counted upon seeing in these
regions was not.

There are no more than twoscore
dwellings upon Dog Island, and a church
which is little more than a chapel. A
small iron cross tops its low steeple; but
this, we knew, was not our quarry. None
of the inhabitants could afford us any information; most of those we questioned
merely stared and shook their heads in
silence. Therefore we strolled down to
the shore and sat disconsolately upon the
rocks by the water-side and gazed across
the bay towards the neat little town, bank-
ed solidly upon the slope of the purpling
hill and looking for all the world as bright
as if it had been new scrubbed that morn-

ing. Thatcher idly tossed a few pebbles into the curling sea.

" It strikes me," I said, presently, being the first to break the silence, " that we have begun poorly. Perhaps that is to be accounted for from the fact that we have tackled our problem from the wrong end."

" The wrong end ?" repeated Thatcher.

" Yes; I believe we would do better to first locate the spot where stood the *mat*, and trust to fate to point out to us the next step in the puzzle."

" I suppose you are right," returned Thatcher, rising; " but with the Ile aux Chiens lying in plain sight, under our very noses, it was only natural that we should make for it first. I am at least satisfied that there is no landmark-cross on this island to-day. Let us call it a false start and begin over again."

Upon our return from this useless excursion, which had taken up the greater part of the morning, we sat ourselves quietly down, with the official map we had purchased and the tracing of the burned chart laid out side by side upon a table before us. Thereupon we set about our labors methodically, as we ought to have done in the beginning.

A glance at the reproduction of the chart will show that the cross, indicating the location of the *cachette*, lies well away towards the western end of the island. After some consideration it became clear to us that if the whole surface of the island of St. Pierre were divided into three approximately equal parts the cross could lie in the third, and that consequently we need waste no time in searching the central and eastern sections. This simplified matters somewhat. We therefore laid off these proportions with as great an accuracy as possible upon the official map, and we thus found that the district in which we hoped to unearth a fortune was the hilliest and most inaccessible part of the island. This we considered a favorable indication; for it must be clear to all that whosoever concealed the gold would naturally have chosen a spot as remote as possible from the town and from observation.

Having come to these conclusions, there was now, so far as we could determine, nothing left for us to do but set out in search of the emplacement of the *mat*. Thatcher favored spending the afternoon in making inquiries among the older fishermen, and he suggested calling upon M. de Manclay, who, he thought, might remember the *mat* as a landmark of St. Pierre; but my instinct unaccountably opposed me to this plan and inclined me rather towards action, and I argued that the less we talked of our affairs — no matter how few our questions nor how veiled our queries might be—the better for us in the long-run; and I finally persuaded Thatcher to undertake a general skirmish or reconnaissance over the country, convincing him that this might probably be more profitable to us in the end than much questioning of ignorant fisherfolk. And the event proved the wisdom of this course.

We set out upon our exploration immediately after the noonday meal. We toiled up the steep and narrow unpaved streets that lead away from the water front, disputing the road half the time with ox-carts, driven by burly red-sashed Basques, and dog teams that trotted merrily by to the encouragement of bare-footed, brown-faced children. There are few horses in barren St. Pierre; imported fodder comes high.

The day was fine. The sun shone brightly from the pale northern sky—a rare luxury in this region of fogs and storms — and the air was cool and bracing. We felt the blood course vigorously through our bodies, that had lacked the benefit of true exercise for some weeks past. As we picked our way through the town we encountered one of our fellow-passengers of the day before—a fat and jovial advocate — who politely inquired whither we were bound at so swinging a pace. We told him we were making a promenade only, and asked him for an orientation. This he gave us glibly, and closed by urging us to climb *la Grande Vigie*, the highest peak of the island, whence he asserted we should obtain a beautiful view of the sea, and of New-foundland, to the northward; he became eloquent and advised us to lose no time in making the ascent, for a clear day, such as this was, might not be known on the island again for a year. Thereupon, to detain us no longer, he bowed extrava-gantly—we returning as good as we got —and set off townwards, shaking his adi-pose body as he went.

"Do you know," began Thatcher, thoughtfully, as we resumed our march, "this looks to me like the hand of Providence."

"What looks to you like the hand of Providence?" I exclaimed, in surprise.

"Meeting Pépinpierre. I am not superstitious, nor am I inclined to believe much in omens; but when a man pops up out of the ground, so to say, and tells you to go to a certain place—which is in the general region of the very spot we are so anxiously searching for—I think there's more in it than a mere coincidence."

"Bosh!" I said. "I would not climb that hill for a farm to-day, view or no view. The lower peak is good enough for a first attempt. Wait until we get in training before we try the other."

We could plainly see, as we trudged along, these two rocky peaks which form the highest points on the island—the nearer, Le Pin de Sucre, some five hundred feet high, and across a little depression behind it La Grande Vigie, some two or three hundred feet higher, which Pépinpierre had so warmly recommended as a belvedere. I thought one peak a day would be sufficient, even for treasure-hunters, and I wanted to take the nearer and lesser eminence first. But Thatcher had apparently not even listened to my objections, as he strode onward straining his eyes hillward as if he would look into the very bowels of the mountain, for he leaped from his thoughts into conversation, and said, excitedly:

"And did you hear what he called it?—La Grande Vigie—'watch hill,' the 'great watch hill'—the place where they used to watch for ships, I suppose—just the place for a flag-staff or a signal-mast of some kind. More than likely it's the very place we're looking for! And, if you want to know it, that's why I say it looks like the hand of Providence!"

"Rot!" I replied, somewhat impatiently. "The signal-station is on Galantry Head, don't you see?" And I pointed towards the bold headland far across the harbor, which we could now plainly see over the house-tops below us.

"It is *now*," said Thatcher, "but it might not have been a hundred years ago. It seems to me as clear as day that, back in those times, when this island was seesawing between French and British rule, there should have been a watching-place and perhaps a signal-pole on the highest available peak. Those fellows would not watch from Galantry when they could broaden their sphere of observation by fifty square miles by climbing La Grande Vigie. And that's just what Grande Vigie means! Come on!"

Thus Thatcher persisted in his determination to ascend the taller peak, and, for the sake of peace, I surrendered to his whim.

CHAPTER XIV

THE SUMMIT OF AN ISLAND PEAK

LEAVING the town well arear, we struck out across Calvary Hill, where stands the conventional gaunt crucifix, facing seaward (the kind of cross we had hoped to find on l'Ile aux Chiens, and doubtless a counterpart of one that stood there in the early days of the island's settlement), and turned into the Route Iphigénie, a broad, well-laid highway that runs across the island to l'Anse de Savoyard. We followed the road as far as the sailors' monument, then struck off to the right and slashed our way through the underbrush towards the foot-hills. This underbrush was about the only vegetable growth we saw on St. Pierre. It is neither tree nor bush, but a sort of gnarled root, of the pine family, I judge, that clings to the interstices of the rocks, and in some places rises to a height of about two feet from the surface. It must be a hardy plant to thrive on such a stony bed, and it is tough, as we learned to our cost. There was no path, of course; we had to pick our way laboriously over the bowlders, slipping here and there up to our ankles into some little rill or spring that lurked beneath a web of twisted roots and withered foliage. Thatcher's rich and expressive vocabulary of expletives afforded us both considerable relief from time to time, and at intervals we sat ourselves down and rested. For over an hour we struggled along in this way, now pulling ourselves up the face of the mountain and now leaping from cliff to cliff across the tiny valleys that seamed the hill-side; and at each pause for breath we gazed back upon the beautiful panorama behind us—the little town lying far below; the silent harbor, where vessels seemed to glide noiselessly about like toy craft; and, beyond, the great broad ocean, all peaceful and blue, stretching away on every side until it fell into the curtain of the sky. To the north rose the dull cliffage of Newfoundland, bleak and gray-green—yet a streak of companionship in this vast loneliness.

As we neared the summit of La Grande Vigie we obtained a good view of the other islands of the group—Grande Miquelon and Langlade, which rises sheer from the water. But the afternoon was wearing on and no time afforded for view-gazing. We hastened upon our journey in such degree as we could. We had half-circled the peak in easing our ascent, and thus we crawled upon its very summit from the rear. A great gale was blowing there, and we were forced to thrust our heads snugly into our hats and lean forward against the support of the blast.

But the sensation was invigorating and exulting, and the view well worthy the efforts we had made to obtain it. We felt under obligations to our friend Pépinpierre.

The summit of this peak looks exceedingly pointed and sharp when seen from the sea or from the town below. This is due to the fact that the topmost part of the eminence is formed of one huge rock that juts upward some fifteen or twenty feet, naked, out of a scramble of lesser bowlders and moss and gnarled roots. The platform of its summit extends no more than half a dozen square yards, sloping off steeply on the Langlade side, but dropping abruptly and perpendicularly where it faces the town and the harbor. Upon the edge of this declivity we sat and swung our legs to the winds over the face of the cliff, and after much strife with the gale we succeeded in lighting our pipes.

" There's one thing sure," said I, when I had regained my breath; "the fellow who lugged his treasure up here to hide it was a duffer."

" Either he was a duffer," admitted Thatcher, "or he needed exercise, and had lots of time—"

" Or mighty little gold !"

"Yes, or mighty little gold," he repeated, pensively; and then we sat there for some minutes and gazed out silently over the sea.

When we had well rested of our ascent, we began to look about us and to examine the surface of the elevation upon which we sat. It was rough and ribbed with clefts and crevices, and spotted here and there with little patches of green and yellow moss.

" There is no indication, so far as I can see, of there ever having been a mast or signal - pole up here," observed Thatcher. " To withstand the gales that must whistle over this peak, a flag-pole would have to be a pretty stout one, and it would need some mighty solid supports."

" Indeed it would," said I; " but let us climb down to the foot of this pedestal and see what there is, and then let's put for home; it's getting late."

We slid cautiously down the incline and scrambled carefully around the base of the huge rock, stumbling over roots and sharp branches to the peril of our clothing. Thatcher was in the van, and he first turned the corner that brought him upon the little plateau which formed a sort of shelf in front of the perpendicular face of the cliff. The gale was crying aloud at this point and conversation was almost impossible, and although from where I stood panting I could plainly see him, I could hear no word he spoke.

Accordingly, I thought he had fallen suddenly demented when I saw him throw his arms violently into the air and leap about like a wild man, his face distorted and strange sounds issuing from his throat. His hat fell to the ground and rolled away a toy to the winds, curling in the air and bobbing from bowlder to bowlder down the hill-side, and his hair, freed of restraint, waved in disorder, giving his countenance a fierce and uncouth appearance. I was spellbound for a brief space and then hastened to his side. He was still shouting incoherently, and when I drew near he seized me by the arm and pointed excitedly to a large iron band welded into the face of the rock. I, too, then felt the thrill that had shot through Thatcher, but with me the outward expression of feeling took another and entirely opposite form, for all I could do was to gasp and lean heavily against the rocky wall in silence. My sensations were similar to those that had welled up in me the day we located the island in the directory at the Hôtel Martin in New York, only

I THOUGHT THATCHER HAD GONE MAD

fiercer, a hundredfold. The gale buzzed in my ears and I heard nothing for some seconds, but soon I was brought to a realization of my surroundings again by a flood of hilarious profanity from Thatcher.

When we had somewhat recovered from this first explosion of our astonishment and joy, we examined the iron fastening more closely. It was very rusty, and in some parts the metal had caked deeply and had fallen away; nevertheless, the heavy band—some half an inch thick and almost two inches wide — was firm and solid in its hold upon the cliff, and bowed outward in the form of a rude semicircle, standing some eighteen inches from the stone at the most distant point. It was fixed in the rock at the height of our shoulders, and there could be no possible doubt from its formation, and from the markings on the face of the cliff, that here had stood, at some time, a pole, held firmly in place by this band.

A further and more careful examination brought new cries of joy to our lips, for we found, about four feet lower down, the remains of a similar brace or band that had apparently long ago been bent back and broken.

" Is there any doubt in your mind about what this is?" asked Thatcher, wildly, as he rose to his feet again from examining the remnants of the lower brace.

" It certainly looks very much as if we had struck something!" I shouted back.

" My boy," he cried, " we are standing within twenty-five yards of a fortune!" and he waved his hand across the horizon. " That gold is almost in our clutches!"

" If it is not already in somebody's else," I said.

"Oh, shut up!" he retorted, roughly, turning upon me. " Don't spoil the delight of these moments. We may have started badly this morning, but we've brought the afternoon to a glorious close."

" I *do* feel hopeful," I said.

" Of course you do. Then don't croak! What did I tell you about the hand of Providence? Do you believe now I had reason to feel that way?"

" I wish I were a more pious man," I said. But Thatcher only laughed hysterically and pounded me on the back.

The sun was now hanging low over a cloud-bank in the west, and we knew we must hasten from the mountain before darkness fell or we might become lost. A few last glances at the iron bands—unimportant bits of rust to all the world but us — and we turned away from the summit of La Grande Vigie, picking our way down the steep, stony hill-side towards the hazy town below us. As we sat in the Café du Midi an hour later, Thatcher, with a tall glass full of a pale-green fluid before him, leaned across the marble - topped table, and, placing his hand on mine, said, with a chuckle of content:

"All the same, old man, this is pretty good work for our first day in St. Pierre." And, all things considered, it was.

CHAPTER XV

A PROBLEM IN GEOMETRY

WE had confidently counted upon finding the *Merry Madge* anchored in the
barachois, or inner harbor, when we
strolled down to the port the next morning, but our expectations were not ful-
filled.   The broad ocean heaved lazily in
the offing under a windless pall of mist,
and a fleet of clumsy luggers hung flap-
ping helplessly in the channel.   Doubtless McLeod lay below the horizon somewhere, whistling for a breeze, and until his
arrival with our reinforcements there was
little for us to do.   But the atmosphere
of St. Pierre made us almost content to
rest upon our oars.   Idleness in a French
town is never irksome, and so we whiled

away that Saturday pleasantly enough, albeit our minds were in no sense upon the dalliance of the hour.

On Sunday morning, when again we looked for the *Merry Madge*, she had not arrived, nor did she appear in the afternoon. We began to grow somewhat impatient, not to say apprehensive. But on Monday morning, when we walked down to the quay, one of the first men we met was Captain John McLeod.

"We had regular fisherman's weather all the way," he explained, as we shook hands all around. "But I don't suppose the delay makes any difference to you?"

"It's just as well you got here," answered Thatcher. "We may not want to stay longer than a week now. Where are you tied up?"

"I'm anchored," said the captain, and as this point in the conversation had brought us opposite to a little building, over the door of which appeared the legend, "*Assurance Contre la Soif*," we stepped inside and sat down and effected insurance. McLeod told us of his trip across from Cape Breton. It seems that all went well enough until the schooner got becalmed the second day out, and that afternoon Carquemort turned up drunk for his watch. He was not wholly incapacitated for work, but he was sullen and stubborn, and came very nearly being insubordinate when McLeod went into the fo'c'sle and found Semsen with the bottle that Carquemort had nearly emptied.

"I took it away from him and chucked it overboard," continued McLeod; "but I tell you, now: I don't hook to that Crackmug fellow, and there never was any good in a Finn. Howsomever, we got along all right when the wind came up — and I guess we'd 'a' got along all right anyhow."

The conversation turned to the unloading of the schooner, and it was decided that this should be done within the next two days, in order that the *Merry Madge* might be at our disposal by that time if we should be ready. Our Frenchmen and the rest of the crew having remained aboard the schooner, which lay in the outer harbor, Thatcher and I took a boat and rowed out to the anchorage, while McLeod made arrangements for docking.

Chiffard was truly delighted to see us, but Carquemort's welcome was somewhat tempered with a suspicion that we had perhaps secured all the gold since our arrival, and had stowed it away to his spoliation. We led the way into the little cabin, and all four sat down to the narrow table under the skylight, the Frenchmen eager and aglow with curiosity, while Thatcher affected an air of mystery which seemed only to increase Carquemort's ill-concealed anxiety. In as few words as possible we told them of our ascent of La Grande Vigie, and of the discovery of the iron rings welded into the rock.

"*C'est bien ça le mat!*" cried Chiffard, almost beside himself. "*Et la cachette, vous l'avez trouvée?*"

We were forced to admit that we had not, and Thatcher sternly bade both men remain quiet until he could explain the situation to them and show just what remained to be done. In order to make this plainer, he produced a rough sketch which he had made the night before, and laid it out upon the table before us.

"Here you have the island of St. Pierre," he said, "and the small island to the right of it, marked B, is l'Ile aux Chiens. We are taking it for granted now that the rock we came upon yesterday is the place where the *mat*, mentioned on Carquemort's chart, originally stood. We will call this spot A. Now then, the chart-maker laid out a straight line from A to some point on B that we are unable to locate; but we know for certain that the landmark he took was on the island B.

It was neither to the north of it nor to the south of it, to the east of it nor to the west of it. Therefore if we lay out a line A C as one limit of the space within which the cross he mentions could have been, and

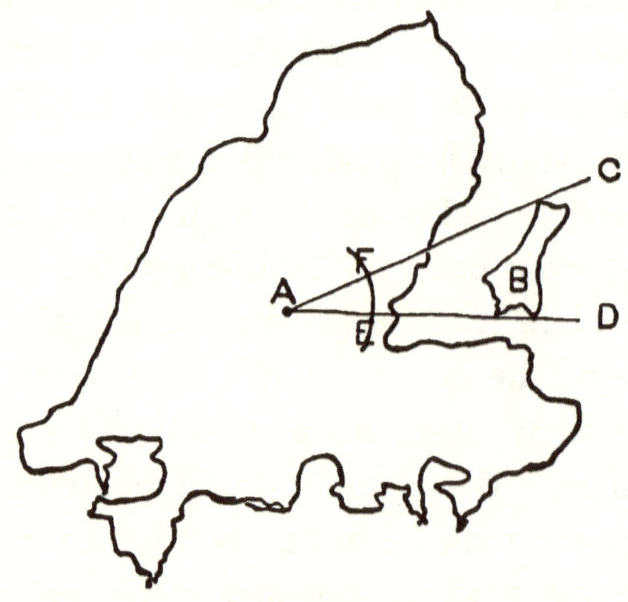

another line A D as the other limit, we enclose on St. Pierre a narrow area within which the *cachette* must lie."

Carquemort could not understand this at first, but Thatcher drew other diagrams, with pictures of poles and crosses and other scenery, so that the man finally got it through his stupid head.

" Now," continued Thatcher, "we know that the treasure was concealed at a point twenty - five paces from A.   Therefore, if we measure off twenty-five paces, A E, on A D, and twenty-five paces, A F, on A C, and describe the arc E F, that arc passes over the *cachette !*"

This last mathematics, however, were too much for our sailorman and cook, as I had warned Thatcher that they would be; but finally, after much talking, we made it clear to them that l'Ile aux Chiens, as seen from La Grand Vigie, looks very small, and that imaginary lines drawn from the rock to the extremities of the island would still be very close together even at twenty-five paces from the apex of the triangle; and that consequently the arc, when described, must fortunately be a small one.   As soon as we had made them understand this, they wanted to land at once and climb the hill, and lay out the survey and fall to with shovel and pick. We were no less anxious to get to work than they, but we had made the ascent of the hill, and we knew what lay before us ; consequently we persuaded the men to dine first and to meet us at one o'clock on the quay, bringing with them a pick each. This much accomplished, we rowed back to the town, crossing McLeod on the way, and delaying long enough to inform him of the orders we had left with the men. These suited him well enough, for he had found he could not dock until the morrow.

Chiffard and Carquemort were awaiting us when we came down to the water-front from our lodgings. They had the picks in a huge sack which, during the ascent of La Grande Vigie, they took turns in carrying. The only impediments we brought were a small telescope that Thatcher had borrowed from a junkman of the village, a ball of thick twine, along a section of which we had measured twenty-five paces, and half a dozen sharp pine stakes for markers.

The day was not so clear as Saturday had been, and by the time we were half-way to the top of the hill the village was almost hidden in a light haze that came floating in from the sea; the sun was clouded, but there was little wind, and, the wise-acres had told us, no prospect of a heavy fog coming on before night to bewilder us in the mountain. Poor Chiffard snorted and perspired as he clambered up the steeps, and cast imprecations upon the head of the *muffle* who had chosen such an unheard-of place to hide his treasure. Carquemort was perfectly taciturn; I believe he expected to find at the summit evidence that Thatcher and I had already done away with the gold; and I have no doubt that if he had he would unhesitatingly have done away with us.

The sight of the rusty iron bands when we reached the summit threw the two men into renewed excitement, and they were unwilling to sit down even for a brief space to rest from the exertions of the ascent. But this they were compelled to do, for their picks were of little avail unless they knew in what spot to dig, and of this Thatcher refused to give any information until he had smoked a pipe within the shelter of the cliff. During this respite he demonstrated practically to our followers the geometry he had been trying to make them understand in the cabin of the *Merry Madge* earlier in the day, and we were even surprised ourselves to note how very small an arc it would be necessary to describe, l'Ile aux Chiens appearing almost insignificant in the glimpses we managed to catch of it through the rifts in the haze.

The measurements were rapidly made as soon as we set about our work.

Thatcher lay at full length on the top of the rock and took the upper end of l'Ile aux Chiens through his telescope, while I, holding one end of the measured twine, the other being fastened to the lower iron band, stood off twenty-five paces and drove a pine stake into the hill-side at the spot indicated by the surveyor. The same method was pursued to lay out the line to the lower extremity of the distant isle, and after that it was a simple matter to describe the necessary arc, driving stakes every few feet. Carquemort and Chiffard thought we must be off in our mathematics; however, this did not deter them from wanting to begin digging at once.

CHAPTER XVI

A DAY OF TOIL

IT will be remembered that the instructions on Carquemort's chart were to the effect that, after pacing off twenty‑five steps from the *mat*, something was to be done with a stone, prior to digging; or perhaps it was intended that some digging was to be done with relation to the position of a certain rock.   This part of the sentence we had been unable to restore, and had counted upon deriving inspiration for our actions from the lay of the land at twenty-five paces from the flag-pole, when we should have found the *mat*.   There was little inspiration to be derived from that hill-top, however, for it consisted almost entirely of huge bowlders scattered

pell-mell one upon another, most of the
rocks weighing many tons. Therefore
we determined, after a careful survey of
the premises, to clear a space for a width
of a few feet, along the arc we had laid
out, of all stones that could be moved by
means of such tools as we had at our disposal, and to frame our future course in
regard to the larger rocks as conditions
might suggest.

The four of us set to work forthwith,
but the labor was by no means a light task,
and dusk was upon us before we had half
completed it. We were consequently
forced to leave it unfinished and return to
the village, after concealing our picks
under a tuft of dwarf pine. We felt no
anxiety of their being stolen during our
absence, and we doubted even if any St.
Pierrese would climb to the top of La
Grande Vigie at any time during the next
month—or during the year, for that matter; but we wished to take every precau-

tion that the suspicions of the natives might not be aroused. What we feared most in the future was that the daily ascent of the mountain by us, strangers, would soon be noticed and commented upon, and perhaps eventually investigated. But we subsequently got around this obstacle by giving out that Thatcher was painting a picture—a view of St. Pierre from the mountain - side. The only unpleasant feature of this fabrication was that we had to carry a box of alleged artist's materials up the ·mountain at our every excursion; but the box usually contained more palatable delicacies than oil-paints, and as no one ever asked to see the fabled picture, we felt that our ruse had been successful with the simple-minded fisherfolk.

The next morning, Tuesday, we were on La Grande Vigie by ten o'clock, Carquemort and Chiffard joining us about half an hour later, as we had made them take a roundabout road of approach—our constant effort being to avoid attracting attention to our movements, or our relations with these men. Our tools were augmented by a crow-bar, a small sledge-hammer, and two spades, but even with these additional aids it took us the entire day to clear away the shrubs and rocks that lay in the small territory under investigation. By the time we knocked off, however, there were only five bowlders of too great a size to be moved, even by our combined efforts, and we left it until the morrow to determine against which we should aim our first serious attack.

At the council we held that evening in the café, Chiffard urged the use of dynamite at once upon all the rocks, this plan being warmly seconded by Carquemort. The latter even volunteered to place the explosives and to ignite the fuses. But we demurred strongly to this, more on account of the danger of discovery than for any other reason, for we feared that even if we waited until a stormy night the explosion of five dynamite cartridges, or of a single one, distant as the mountain-top was, would startle the French government for a certainty, and probably result in a search into the cause of such an unusual detonation that must redound to our discomfiture. I finally suggested that we select the rock most likely to be the one we wished to dislodge, for we had concluded that the treasure was probably under or near one of the five great rocks, and dig around its base to a depth of several feet. My contention was that if a bowlder had been placed over the *cachette*, we should thus make sure of that fact by digging to its base, whereas if the bowlder were not the one mentioned in the chart it would probably extend to a considerable depth below the surface, having been a feature of the landscape at the time the treasure was buried. The event proved that this plan was a wise plan, for it did away with the use of explosives and led us to make the discovery we had travelled so far to attempt.

We started in at the same hour the following morning, Wednesday, upon the labor of displacing the rock nearest the centre of the space we had cleared. The work was of the hardest kind we had yet been forced to undertake, for the bowlder was wedged in by a quantity of smaller rocks—small by comparison only—weighing on an average from 400 to 500 pounds each. These we had first to loosen in their beds and then, by the severest kind of exertion, lift out of their emplacements and roll away. It was only possible for three of us to work at a time, it having been considered wisest for one man to remain constantly on watch against the approach of strangers. This method, however, had the advantage of affording to each one of us a chance for rest at frequent intervals. By dusk we had cleared a ditch some two feet deep half-way around the great stone. We must have handled several tons of porphyry that day. And the exertion proved too much for us, for on the following morning both Thatcher and I were entirely played out —lame, stiff, and sore—and we determined that this day should be taken for rest. I think Chiffard and Carquemort were not displeased at the announcement.

In this manner we also secured an opportunity to have some intercourse with Captain McLeod, whom we had scarcely seen since the day of his arrival; and when we learned that the *Merry Madge* was now unloaded and prepared to take on cod as soon as we gave the word, we bade our skipper wait until Monday, when we hoped to be able to give him some definite information concerning our future plans.

It so happened, however, that we went

aboard of the *Merry Madge* hastily the following evening and, by force of circumstances, confided to McLeod the complete facts concerning our enterprise. As a result, the little schooner found herself, early Saturday morning, anchored in l'Anse de Savoyard—a little bay on the southern coast of the island — and we then entered upon one of the most thrilling labors that I ever was, or expect to be, called upon to perform during my life. But I am anticipating.

CHAPTER XVII

THE SECRET OF THE CHART

We rested all day Thursday, as I have said, and on Friday morning, at the usual hour, we were again at our rock-digging with renewed strength and energy. The day was quite foggy and the town below was completely hidden from our view—and we from the people's!—but we had now become so familiar with the path of ascent and descent that we no longer feared becoming lost in the mist. Consequently, we were pleased with the weather conditions, and all worked steadily and persistently at lifting bowlders and rolling them from their beds down into the bush-grown clefts of the hill-side below us.

It must have been shortly after midday, and just about time for us to knock off work to sample the contents of Thatcher's "paint-box," that the famous discovery was made which resulted in leaving the "paint-box" unopened until five o'clock that afternoon. Chiffard was knee-deep in the ditch that we had dug around the big bowlder, puffing and groaning with a crow-bar, when the thing slipped and was swallowed almost to its entire length into the hill-side. The cook fell flat, of course, and bruised himself, and what he said would not look well in print. I believe, however, that the man was more frightened than hurt, for he scrambled out of the ditch and called loudly upon Thatcher and me, who were laboring like a pair of Sisyphi at rolling a huge rock. When we came to him and he explained what had happened, pointing out to us only a few inches of the handle of the crow-bar above ground, we realized that he had struck some kind of a hole,

and the hope that it might be the *cachette*
threw us again into one of those frenzies
of excitement that had overwhelmed us
on one or two previous occasions in connection with our hunt for buried treasure.

Thatcher leaped into the ditch and
withdrew the crow-bar. Then he fell
upon his knees, and with some difficulty
forced his hand and forearm into the
crevice through which the tool had fallen.

" This must be the place!" he shouted,
presently. " I can't feel anything below,
but there is certainly a large chamber of
some kind here! I can feel the top—it
seems to be a flat stone!"

Then he made way for me, and I thrust
my arm in and felt about in the dark hollow, and afterwards both Chiffard and
Carquemort did likewise. The two latter
were almost beyond control, and Carquemort, in his eagerness to tear away the
rocks near the aperture, labored fiercely
with his fingers until they bled. When,

after a few moments, we had all become almost rational again, and had made a closer and more careful examination of the crevice, we concluded from such general indications as were evident that Chiffard, by a fortunate hazard, had sent his crow-bar into a hole some two or three feet deep, over the top of which rested a flat stone. The bar had entered just under the edge of this stone, and by removing some smaller bowlders in a new direction from that in which we had been working, we found that the flat rock was about three feet long in one of its dimensions. Piled above it were stones and earth and roots some two feet deep— an accumulation of years, doubtless, and probably an artifice of concealment as well.

"If this is the *cachette*," said Thatcher, as he wiped great beads of perspiration from his brow, "we have come upon it from the side, and this flat rock closes the upper orifice. There is no necessity for removing all that stuff on top. Let us now widen the little opening we have already made until we can see or reach inside of the vault."

But this was not so easy of accomplishment as our enthusiasm could have desired; nevertheless excitement lent us the power of Titans, and at the end of an hour we had torn away a couple of stones that formed a part of the side wall of the hiding-place. Then, by the aid of lighted matches, we saw that we had come upon some sort of an artificial chamber about two cubic yards in capacity. What the chamber contained, however, we could not then ascertain; but that this was the *cachette* we no longer entertained the slightest doubt. An hour more of persistent work and we had broken an opening about two feet square, through which it was decided that one of us must thrust his head and shoulders, while the others held him by the heels, to investigate the interior of the dark chamber. The part of imitating Israel Putnam fell to me, being the smallest man of the four, and I must confess that it was with considerable reluctance, barely tempered by the hope of bringing gold to light, that I finally consented to push my head into that black hole where there might be lurking some strange kind of danger, the nature of which, of course, I was unable to imagine, for I knew there were no snakes on the island of St. Pierre.

First, I placed my right arm through the orifice and felt about in the darkness, and then I lay down upon my stomach and worked my head slowly under the stones, while a shower of pebbles and dirt rattled over my face and down my neck, and the jagged side of the rocks tore my hair. Carquemort and Thatcher held me firmly by the feet, and Chiffard jabbered volubly in helpless idleness. When I had worked my head and shoulders well within the chamber my hand touched bottom, and I could feel stones of all sizes, or what I at first thought to be stones; but the large ones seemed all to be of about the same size and smooth, and after a few seconds of careful feeling I was aware that they were square and seemingly arranged in some order. I felt confident then that what I touched was not stone, but gold or silver—surely metal of some kind in bullion—and although I burned to give an expression to the feelings that arose in me, I soon found that a man almost throttled in a black, airless pit is physically unequal to rise to such an occasion. But I signalled wildly with my heels to be pulled out, and when finally my companions got me to the surface again my clothes were torn, my face and head were bleeding, and I felt as if I were almost suffocated. All I could say was:

"Gold! *De l'or, mes amis!* Gold bars!"

In spite of the fact that we had labored for so many weeks to find this *cachette*, and would have experienced the bitterest disappointment if we had never discovered it—or, if found, it had been empty—none of the three—Thatcher, Carquemort, or Chiffard — would believe that what I said was true; and even I myself, after a few seconds of daylight, doubted my own senses. So it came that I was almost forced into the jagged hole again, with injunctions to bring out the gold if it was really there! But after almost bursting every blood-vessel in my head, I kicked for rescue once more, and when dragged back to the fresh air had only succeeded in partially dislodging one of the heavy square pieces of metal that lay embedded in the bottom of the chamber.

In spite of the protestations and entreaties of the others, I swore that I would not go into that place again that day, and I lay down upon the hill-side to recover from my efforts. Carquemort fell at once to an attack upon the rocks with the sledge, but Chiffard and Thatcher plied me with questions — and brandy — and were soon themselves executing a war-dance that appeared to me, played out as I was, wholly undignified and superfluous. I shouted to them that they would do better to thrust their heads into the pit and derive experience, but they laughed at me, and Chiffard bawled the most absurd statements concerning what he intended to do with his money when he got back to New York.

No further progress did we make that day, for night was approaching. We rolled a bowlder over the opening we had made, and concealed our tools and groped our path down the mountain-side almost in darkness, guided by the twinkling lights of the town and by the great revolving flash on Galantry Head.

We dined that night on the best there

was to be had in St. Pierre — including the driest of champagne, that had never paid duty!—and Chiffard left the straight and narrow path and caroused so with that beast of a Carquemort that the quiet streets rang with their vociferations, until a patrolling gendarme seized them and threw them bodily on board of the *Merry Madge*, that lay moored at the quay.

Thither, too, in our exuberance, did we find our way; and we saw our allies sprawling upon the forward hatch. We awakened McLeod and bound him by great oaths to secrecy, and told him of our adventure, for we knew he must eventually be intrusted with our confidence; and although he thought we were foolish with wine and were telling him a prodigious yarn to shield some baser undertaking, he listened discreetly and fell in with our desires like the true man that he was.

From La Grande Vigie we had noticed

a little bay which juts into the base of the hill on the far side from the town, and at a lesser distance.   McLeod told us this was l'Anse de Savoyard, a convenient anchorage, especially for the loading of the quality of cod he expected to buy.   Here, for the first time, our Scot intimated that the cargo he intended to carry away would be in bottles and casks rather than of quintals of salted fish ; and as the purposes of all concerned would therefore be the better served by a greater privacy, it was agreed that the *Merry Madge* should put into l'Anse de Savoyard early the following morning.

Thus it was that, shortly after daylight, when Chiffard and Carquemort were brought to consciousness by the heaving of the schooner as she bobbed over the waves before a spanking breeze, tacking out to sea, with Galantry fading on the starboard quarter, the two men thought we had bribed McLeod to kidnap them ;

and, in their momentary fury, it is probable that slaughter was only averted by bring-ing the *Merry Madge* about and pointing her for the headland, behind which she cast anchor an hour later in the snug little bay of Savoyard.

CHAPTER XVIII

FORTUNES FOR FOUR

ALTHOUGH McLeod put no faith in the tale of buried treasure we had spun for him in the middle of the night, he felt confident we had succeeded in whatever enterprise had led us to the lonely shores of St. Pierre, and expressed himself as willing to assist us in any way possible in what remained to be done. The fisher-men who lived in the huts along the edge of the cove, he said, had been of service to him before, and understood perfectly the nature of the business that brought the *Merry Madge* to so secluded an anchorage. This was good news for us, for we had feared we might have some difficulty in smuggling our booty on board. We therefore bade our skipper load his " cod " with expedition, and ourselves, with Carquemort and Chiffard, again sought the mountain-top.

The morning was spent in the Herculean task of enlarging the aperture we had already made under the flat stone, and by noon we had succeeded in making it broad enough for any one of us to enter the chamber with head and shoulders so as to be able to work within with both hands. Carquemort was assigned to the task of extracting the first sample of our findings, and the eager expression of his face as he kneeled to carry out this task was almost beastlike in its fierce greed. He heaved and wrestled for some brief moments with the thing I had partially dislodged the previous afternoon, and then slowly squirmed backward and outward, assisted by us all. His hands came forth last from the darkness, and clutched between them was an oblong, yellowish-brown colored object which we all recognized at once as an ingot of solid gold !

As he dropped the heavy burden upon the ground he rolled over and exclaimed, breathlessly:

"*Bon Dieu !   Le trou en est plein !*"

The realization that we now stood face to face with a large fortune—a fortune, even when quartered, sufficient to make each one of us independently rich for the rest of his life—did not affect any of us in the manner that I should have thought it would. We all took the climax more or less calmly; and I suppose this was so because our nerves had been worked up by continuous exciting incidents to a pitch where failure only would have snapped their tension.

The ingot that Carquemort brought to light was oblong in shape, and measured some six inches in length by four in width by two in depth. These figures

are only approximate, for we never actually measured any of the gold bricks.
We weighed two or three that night and
they averaged twenty-eight pounds. But
of this more later on.

As soon as we had satisfied our curiosity and had each examined and fondled
the brick over and over again, Carquemort was sent into the *cachette* to extract
another. He had less difficulty in loosen-
ing the second and those he subsequently
secured, for the earth and pebbles that
had cemented the upper layer of ingots
had not filtered through to encumber the
others. By noon, therefore, we had a
dozen of the bricks piled before us. But
such a profusion of treasure made us cal-
lous to its fascination, and we actually sat
upon the gold as we ate our luncheon at
noon, talking wild and hilarious nonsense
the while. Then, taking turns at the labor, we worked until the sun had fallen
low and over fifty tawny bars had been

recovered, with no indication of there being an end to the supply!

The question of transporting and
guarding so much wealth now arose as a
mighty problem, and we were occupied
for a considerable period in its settlement. It was at length decided that two
of us should remain upon the mountain
all night, and the fortune of lot relegat-
ed this unpleasant duty to Carquemort
and Chiffard. Thatcher and I, however,
agreed to bring up to them warm clothing, sou'westers, food, and drink, but
they were bound not, under any circumstances, to make a light — not even to
smoke — so great had become our fear
of detection.

So, upon this promise, we left them,
carrying in the "paint-box" two of the
bricks. (I commend to any one who desires exercise the carrying down a rough
mountain-side of fifty-six pounds dead
weight.) We reached the shore of the

inlet towards six in the evening, just at dusk, and Glen McLeod came out for us in a dory. The skipper was anxiously watching for our approach over the rail, and we at once invited him into the cabin.

His amazement at sight of our prize was such as I have rarely seen at any time, and when we told him of the pile of similar bars that lay on the top of the mountain he sank back speechless upon the cabin bench. We got the scales from the galley and weighed the two bricks. As I have written, they averaged twenty-eight pounds each, as did several others which we subsequently tested. Thatcher took pencil and paper from his pocket and figured.

" Gold," he said, " is worth about twenty dollars a Troy ounce, if I remember correctly. I doubt, however, if this stuff is pure. American gold coin is over .990 fine. This can't be more than .800 fine, and, at a rough guess, is worth, say, $16.00 to the Troy ounce, or "—and he figured away rapidly—"about $232 to the pound avoirdupois. At any rate, let us figure on that basis. Now, one of these bricks weighs twenty-eight pounds: that would be twenty-eight times two hundred and thirty-two dollars, say $6496. This brick, gentlemen, is worth $6496!"

A dead silence followed that statement, and we each in turn examined Thatcher's figures, that we might be convinced.

"Holy Moses!" said McLeod, as he gazed from one to the other of us, and his was the only open comment.

We supped hastily, and as we ate we decided not to leave the schooner with $13,000 of our gold unguarded. McLeod, knowing we were to return to our fellow-millionaires, had asked to be taken up to La Grande Vigie that he might see the treasure of his own eyes, and so Thatcher and he set off to carry comfort to our

Frenchmen, while I remained in the cabin with the treasure.

The next morning, early, I climbed the hill alone, leaving Thatcher to watch aboard the *Merry Madge*, and the day was spent in carrying down the gold bars, four at a time, in sacks. The process was necessarily slow and fatiguing, but we all got long rests between journeys by taking turns in guarding the schooner and the *cachette*. This method kept two of us continually idle, which, in a sense, was a disadvantage. The most unpleasant duty of the whole process of transferrence was the night-watch on the hill, where the temperature towards dawn frequently fell to freezing, and we could not even allow ourselves the solace of a pipe. Rain, too, for three days made the night misery almost unbearable; but nearly any kind of suffering becomes supportable when one is pulling wealth out of a hole at the rate of about $25,000 to the minute; and so it was that we plugged away steadily and cheerfully for ten days until there was not a bar left in the famous *cachette.* When we were convinced of this we took account upon our check-list and found that we had stowed away in the cabin of the *Merry Madge* no less than five hundred and seventy-seven bars of gold! If this should eventually prove to be worth sixteen dollars an ounce, as Thatcher had calculated, we were now the possessors of $3,747,092! Three million seven hundred and forty-seven thousand and ninety-two dollars! Think of it!—$936,773 for each one of us nineteenth-century adventurers!

But here is no place to drag into ecstasies over our riches; and my tale is already stretching far beyond the limit I had set at the beginning. Brevity seems to be a virtue that this story has lacked thus far, but I trust the truth of the statements will atone for the verbiage. I find that when writing of things one has done and seen, it is a task to thresh detail.

In all this time of gold-digging Carquemort had been the one to seem not wholly satisfied with our fortune. His constant talk was of more, more, more! He would exclaim, as he mouthed the figures of our calculations, how fortunate the man would be who could own all we had found; and at times he broke into curses upon Chiffard, grudging the cook his share—poor Chiffard, who had worked hard from the start, and who, after all, had been the means of bringing Carquemort to us and of thus making it possible for him to secure the solution of the mystery of his half-burned chart.

Thus it was that when the rest of us were satisfied and convinced that no more treasure lay within the *cachette*, Carquemort still brooded over the possibility of finding more if we should dig deeper, and, to be just towards him, his contention was certainly more or less warranted by the wording of the chart which said "*pièces et lingots*," we having supplied the last word, and correctly as the event had proved. For we had dug out of the *cachette* over three million dollars in ingots, but no coin. Neither Thatcher nor I believed there could be any coin there, as a very thorough search of the pit had been made by each one of us after the withdrawal of the last ingot, and we felt disinclined to waste time in digging about any more, being anxious to escape from the little cove of Savoyard with the booty we had before an evil chance should betray our enterprise to the government of the island, and so compel us to surrender a large portion, if not all, of our treasure. McLeod, too, was apprehensive about further delay, for gossip flies swiftly in small places, and there were many tongues that could wag to ill purpose concerning the "cod" in the hold of the

Merry Madge. Furthermore, we had promised the good skipper one bar out of our great plenty as his share in the success of the venture, and so the canny Scot, with his mental eye fixed upon $6496, was doubly eager to see Galantry drop below the horizon in the wake of the *Merry Madge.*

Carquemort was so persistent, however, that we agreed to devote one full day additional to La Grande Vigie to satisfy him that there was no more gold to be had; and upon this concession he agreed to offer no further objection to an early departure thereafter. This understanding was reached on the evening of Tuesday, August 10th, that being the date upon which we brought down the last bars from the summit. Our plan as projected then was to slip quietly out of the cove at dark the following evening, August 11th, with, doubtless, the richest cargo that ever left St. Pierre.

CHAPTER XIX

THE LAST LOAD

Thus, in spite of the fact that I had thought we had all seen the last of La Grande Vigie, three of us found ourselves upon the summit again, hidden in fog, the next morning—Thatcher remaining on guard aboard ship. The tools lay in the bottom of the *cachette* undisturbed, as we had left them the day before, and after they had been removed Carquemort announced that he intended to enter the chamber bodily. This we had none of us undertaken previously, having recovered the treasure by merely diving into the hole, while those without clung to the worker's feet. Yet, now that all the gold had been taken out, it was barely possible that the *cachette* would accommodate a man, but I could not see that space enough would be left to enable him, once inside, to use his arms for work of any kind, especially Carquemort, awkward, hulking seaman that he was. But he slid in nevertheless, feet first, and Chiffard muttered to me under his breath that he would like nothing better than to roll a bowlder up against the opening of the *cachette* and leave the ruffian to his fate. That we did not do this is only one more proof to my mind that morality, after all, is but a mere engine of Providence, which makes me reflect further that a century and a half ago, when there was precious little morality, the plans of Providence must have been fearfully interfered with; all of which rather obtuse and complicated philosophy will be the better understood at the close of this tale.

There was better accommodation inside of that *cachette* than I had supposed, for Carquemort could be heard grunting and scuffling about within to a staccato accompaniment of falling pebbles, while Chiffard and I sat outside in the fog and smoked. He was digging with his knife at the bottom of the pit, and he kept at this persistently for almost two hours, in spite of our offers to take his place for a time and our taunts that he was wasting his energy in an empty black hole.

At the end of that period, however, the tables were entirely turned, and the laugh rested wholly with Carquemort; and, to say truth, I believe he was the most surprised of the three. To put it briefly, when he had dug some six or eight inches down into the hard clay which had compacted at the bottom of the *cachette*, his knife-point struck sparks, and a little more scraping proved that in the bottom of the pit lay a large iron-clamped chest. Of course we each took turns of inspection at once, and the blackguarding we got from Carquemort meanwhile was such as would have ranked the foulest-worded of Captain Kidd's crew as a drawing-room conversationalist.

I, being the smallest of stature, was next allowed to slide into the pit, and to my surprise I found that I could lean over and cut away the clay in reasonable comfort. The refuse was passed up to the surface in our caps and thrown out; and when it came Chiffard's turn to labor, fully one-third of the lid of the strong-box had been cleared to view. An hour or so after that the top of the chest was free, yet the chest itself was still so firmly embedded as to be immovable. The work progressed slowly, both because of the difficulty of attack and because we could use jack-knives only; but towards mid-afternoon we had hacked away enough sediment from one side of the chest to clear the lock. This Carquemort smashed with the crow-bar after a good fifteen minutes of volcanic profanity, and the snapping of the bolts was soon followed by an eruption of gold and silver coins that he tossed to us from within, clambering out immediately himself with his two fists full of doubloons. I say doubloons, and I have no doubt that such they were, for they were gold pieces, big and heavy; and although many were badly rubbed, there were enough stamped with the profiles of kings and bearing pious legends to identify the famous gold piece of pirate story-books. There were silver coins, too, and larger and smaller gold pieces, and a few coppers — the latter all French, as was also much of the gold and silver. I regretted that as a boy I had never collected coins, that I might have known these pieces by name and nation; but one thing I was sure of, and that was their genuineness and their great value and unquestioned age, for no date did we find greater than 1740, and only a few of these, all fresh coins. We were more affected by this find than we had been by the bullion, for the money appealed more directly to our sense of sight and appreciation than did the tawny bricks. Chiffard and Carquemort again and again held the coins high in air and let them sift through their fingers and fall into a jingling pile upon the ground below, and I found myself compelled to use hard words and some physical force to keep Carquemort from stuffing his pockets. Finally I ordered him away, on the pretext that he go to the schooner and fetch rope and a pair of oars, or boat-hooks, and some flour-bags in which to carry off our treasure.

While he was gone I entered the *cachette* and passed out capful after capful of gold and silver pieces to Chiffard until my back and arms fairly ached, and the cook piled all these in a great stack on his coat that had been spread out near by.

The box I was delving from was about half the size of an ordinary modern steamer trunk. This may give some idea of what its capacity was, and this capacity was taxed to the utmost, for when I first lifted the lid the coins were brim even. The pile outside, as I saw it when I emerged, was fully two feet high and almost three feet in diameter at the base. What the actual value of all this was in money of to-day I cannot state, for it was never satisfactorily computed; but Thatcher, who proved himself the mathematician and financier of the expedition, divided the silver coins from the gold the night we sailed from St. Pierre and made a rough estimate of the contents of the chest, which he reckoned at nearly $200,-000. This brought our grand total up to nearly four millions of dollars.

To return to our day's work, however. Carquemort got back from the schooner at just about sunset. The coins had all

WE CARRIED OUR COINS DOWN IN BASKETS

been recovered and Chiffard was in the *cachette* trying to dislodge the chest, for we thought we might find about it some clew to the source of all this wealth, and, incidentally, to the designer of our luckful chart. Carquemort brought with him a pair of oars and some rope but no bags, for of these he had been able to get none. Thus it became imperative that we dig out the chest, for we had nothing else in which to carry away the money. We did finally dislodge it, and after much trouble we pulled it through the aperture to the surface. It was too dark by that time to make any examination, and beyond noting that it was an unusually strong oaken box, bound and clamped with iron, I paid little attention to it. The coins were poured back into it and shaken down so that we could close the lid, and the coffer was then stoutly bound with rope, with nooses arranged so that it could be slung on the oars and carried by two of us. But when we came to attempt this we found that by our united efforts we were only just capable of raising the great weight a few inches from the ground.

The result was another night's watch on La Grande Vigie, the lot falling this time to Carquemort and me, and the next day, in four tiresome trips, we carried our coins down to the cove in cod-baskets. Each load was dumped into the chest, that had gone aboard carrying the first instalment, and was stowed for greater safety in the bunk of the little cabin where one of us had expected to sleep during the return trip. Thus, finally, our entire hoard was put into the *Merry Madge*, and nothing further held us to St. Pierre. The capstan began clinking at eight o'clock that night, and the wind holding fair and southeasterly, the little schooner slipped quietly out of the bay in the darkness just half an hour later.

CHAPTER XX

HOMEWARD BOUND

UP to the present I have said little about Semsen, the fourth hand aboard the *Merry Madge*, whom we shipped at the last hour out of a North Sydney grogshop. It has seemed best to reserve his indictment until he moved more prominently into our story, and that period we have now reached.

He was a Finn, as I think I have told —a lank, greasy beast, fit to sustain the evil repute that hangs at the heels of all those of his race who follow the sea. He worked well enough, it seems, on the trip over from Cape Breton, being in good pay and not yet spoiled by association with Carquemort, although Heaven knows he must have been bad enough from the start. Rum and our black-hearted partner did the rest.

On two or three occasions during the time the schooner lay at anchor in the cove, McLeod had let drop some remark which plainly showed us the fellow was losing favor with the skipper. But even this caused us no particular uneasiness. Semsen had had ten days of almost perfect idleness while we were transferring the treasure, for we never called upon him to assist us, and so far as McLeod's enterprise was concerned, all Semsen had to do was to row the dory back and forth a couple of times in the evening when the kegs and cases came out from the town to Savoyard in little wagons drawn by dogs. It was impossible to keep the man in ignorance of the nature of the schooner's main cargo, and I doubt if concealment was ever attempted in that direction, but he was given pretty plainly to understand that he must keep his mouth shut, and he was not allowed any shore leave. As to the treasure, we tried at first to keep the true nature of the affair from him, but when we continued coming down the hill day after day with our loads of gold bars and clambering clumsily over the rail with them, it seems almost impossible that an inkling of the truth should have failed to sift through his idle brain. As a matter of fact, Carque-mort probably told him all about the whole business soon after the *cachette* was discovered, for we have agreed since, in discussing our adventures, that Semsen, for a man ignorant, showed a remarkable lack of interest in the peculiar proceed-ings he was living in the very midst of. He and Carquemort had been on friendly terms from the start, and every evening the latter was not on duty at the summit of La Grande Vigie the two used to sit in the bow smoking their pipes and talking

in undertones, and their conversation always ceased when Glen McLeod, or
Chiffard, or any other of us approached.
This did not arouse our suspicions at the
time, although, when you consider the
temptation to crime latent in the millions
we had housed in the cabin, I suppose it
should have. Doubtless, during those
long conversations, Semsen and Carquemort concocted the plan which they tried
to put into effect some days later, and
which might very well have succeeded in
spite of their being only two against five
if fortune had not favored us as it did.
What the plan actually was I am also
unable to say with any degree of exactitude, for its development came so suddenly, when it did come, that we were all
taken by surprise. I feel sure, however,
that some part of their scheme went
wrong, or possibly some misunderstanding between the two caused a premature
execution, for it would hardly seem pos-

sible that they should attempt to attack five men in the manner they did. And now, having made this brief exposition of the temper of our treacherous fellows, let us return to the little schooner on the night we put out of l'Anse de Savoyard.

The cove fell quickly out of sight in the darkness, and as we rounded the point we picked up the lights of St. Pierre off the port bow, the night being clear. The wind favored us, and before long the revolving light on Galantry Head had dropped well astern. We went down into the dingy cabin—McLeod, Thatcher, and I. No definite plans had been made as to our port of destination otherwise than that we should head in the general direction of North Sydney and decide as soon as possible exactly where and how we should try to land our gold. We had been too busy up to the present to think about anything further than getting safely away from the French.

On this first night out, however, we postponed any discussion of our plans in order to count the coins that lay in the bunk of the extra cabin. It was a glorious entertainment, in which McLeod took part, and the result of Thatcher's rough calculations was, as I have said, that the value of the coins approximated $200,000.

The most important discovery came later in the evening, after the mathematics had been laid aside, when we set to making the first close examination of the chest. It was an unusually well-made box. The wood was doubtless oak or ash, but we could not be certain on account of its age. The iron clasps and hinges were wrought in curious designs, and the padlock, on the reverse, was decorated with a crown in cameo with these letters engraved in script beneath it, "*N. D. de la D.*" We thought that this would remain our only clew to the identity of the original owner of the strong-box, but McLeod, who possessed sharp eyes, claimed that he could discover the trace of a name on the lid, and we, too, finally managed to recognize signs of lettering. I took a clothes-brush and polished the top of the chest off to the best of my strength, scattering the floor with dirt and rust and bits of wood that fell before the vigor of my assault. Then we wiped the surface with an oiled rag, and thus brought out more clearly the words that had almost faded away. McLeod's eyesight was again brought into requisition and he spelled out "*a Deliv anc.*" Beyond that we could rescue nothing from the darkness.

To us who had labored so long and assiduously over the burned chart the present puzzle proved a simple one, and we made the faded letters at once into "*la Délivrance,*" and coupling this with the letters on the padlock we concluded that the name of the ship to which this chest had originally belonged was "*N. D. de la Délivrance;*" but what "N. D." might stand for we did not then determine, and, to be frank, just at that time we did not much care. Our minds were on other matters, and our hearts set rather into the future than upon the past. So we stowed the coins back again carefully into the box, stacking them according to size, and filling the chinks with cotton-waste; and then we nailed down the lid of the coffer, and after much effort moved it back again into the port cabin, where it formed a sort of step to the bunk.

Just as we were about to turn in for the night Thatcher startled us by leaping to his feet, tearing open the cabin-door and striding up the companion-way three steps at a time. We heard him walk rapidly around the deck and speak a few words to Glen, whose turn it was at the wheel, and then he returned.

"I guess I've got 'em again," was all he said.

"Why? What ailed you?" asked McLeod.

"Why, I looked up there and I could swear I saw a face peering down through the skylight. That man Semsen, I thought. I rushed up to see who it was, but there was no one on deck but Glen at the wheel."

"You need rest," I said; and for the time we thought no more of the incident.

CHAPTER XXI

AN UNEXPECTED OUTBREAK

THE next morning we slept late—that is, late for seafarers—for when I awoke it was half-past seven. McLeod had gone on deck long before. I aroused Thatcher, and as we dressed we could tell from the lazy motion of the schooner and by the groaning and creaking of the booms that the *Merry Madge* was becalmed. Above we found the captain smoking his pipe and saying things that would not look well in print, and he pointed northward to a heavy bank of dull gray clouds flush with the ocean.

"Fog?" said I, for the atmosphere even then was thick and chilly.

"Yes," growled McLeod, "and in an

hour we'll be packed in it like in cotton."

We took our breakfast in the galley with Chiffard, who was whistling jovially over his pots and kettles and forever joking about the condescension it was on his part—a millionaire—to play sea-cook. But he played his part well, and McLeod used to mourn the coming loss of so good a hand at making coffee.

By the time we had finished our scant meal the fog was upon us, and in less than an hour every rope of the rigging was dripping dismally. Thatcher and I had smoked our pipes and were back again in the cabin lounging on the spare bunks, with our feet cocked up on the piles of bullion, discussing the port we had better make for as soon as the wind favored, when we heard heavy foot-falls on the steps, and Carquemort stalked into the cabin.

" Hallo !" exclaimed Thatcher. " How

did you get down here? Where's the captain?"

"The devil take the captain!" retorted Carquemort, sullenly. "I guess I'm as good as he. Do you know I'm getting tired of this dog business? I've got just as much right in this cabin as you have! That money 's as much mine as yours. Where's the chest?"

"See here, Carquemort," said Thatcher, quite calmly, rising, "sit down there."

"I did not come here to sit down," continued Carquemort. "I want some of that money."

"Well, you can't have any of that money," returned Thatcher, sharply. "And if you don't want to listen to reason, you can get right out of here!"

Carquemort was looking about the cabin in search of the chest; but that was safely locked in the port state-room, and I carried the key to the door in my pocket.

"What do you want with money to-day?" I asked, pacifically.

"I want to have it in my pocket. It's mine, and I've a right to it. I want to divide the coin in the chest now. We may hang here in this fog for a week."

"It was understood in the beginning that this treasure was not to be divided until we reached land," I said. "And, what's more, it won't be, either; you may depend upon that! If you have anything reasonable to say, very well; but—"

Here McLeod came down from the deck, and he appeared somewhat surprised at finding the Frenchman in the cabin.

"That will do, Carquemort," said Thatcher, as if dismissing the man, and he sat down again and went at filling his pipe. Carquemort scowled and climbed slowly up the companion-way.

"That fellow's getting ugly," I said.

"Ugly?" repeated McLeod.

" Yes. I guess he has not got enough work to do, captain," put in Thatcher. "Can't you set him at something that will keep him busy until we get under way again ?"

" I guess I can find something to occupy the beast," he said; and after putting on his sou'wester, which he had come down for, he left us again. We heard him bawling some orders above, and there was an interchange of oaths that fairly shook the panes of the skylight.

And now I shall have to tell this part of the story as the events happened, and as they were told to me afterwards, not as I saw them; for, being below, Thatcher and I were not witnesses to what occurred in the beginning of the exciting period that followed Carquemort's visit to the cabin. It seems that McLeod set the Frenchman and Semsen at some sort of dirty labor aloft on the foremast— scraping the top-mast, I believe, though

I'm pretty weak on nauticalities — and Glen was ordered to take the wheel and watch the sails in case a breeze sprang up. Occasionally, too, he blew a mournful blast upon a fog-horn—a perfectly useless proceeding, for we were apparently alone upon the surface of that foggy sea. McLeod sat by, smoking in silence, and Chiffard was busy in the galley. And so things went for half an hour or more, with the drip, drip, drip of the fog upon the deck and the hoarse tooting of Glen's horn as the only disturbance of that ominous peace.

Presently the captain arose and leaned far over the rail, and peered intently into the mist for some moments.

"See here, Glen," he said, "d'ye catch sight of anything beyond?"

Glen strained his eyes for some moments, and replied that he thought he could make out some sort of a dark object floating off the port quarter.

" Yes," said the skipper, " there's somethin' there, sure, and it's floatin' this way. Mayhap it might be a dory or the like;" and, sure enough, that is what it proved to be. It came slowly along on the tide, its outlines growing more and more distinct, and in a few moments it was bobbing, bottom up, almost within reach of the stern of the *Merry Madge*, but still well beyond the grasp of a boat-hook.

" There goes twenty-five dollars, my boy," remarked McLeod.

"What do you let it go for?" asked Glen. " Is she sound?"

" Seems to be," and then, struck with a sudden idea: " Lend a hand there, lad, and we'll have that. Launch a dory, now, lively;" and almost in less time than it takes to tell, the father and son had gotten our smaller dory over the rail—we only carried two, nested over the main hatch—and had shoved off in pursuit of the derelict. Glen sculled with a single oar, while the older McLeod kneeled in the bow, leaning on the boat-hook as though it were a huge harpoon. Fog is a traitor to judgment, or else the tide took a sudden flow, for the two men found they had quite a distance to go before they overhauled the upturned dory.

And now comes the devil-work of that incarnate fiend, Carquemort. Scarcely had McLeod and Glen put off from the schooner when the men dropped their work aloft and tumbled down to deck. Whether they had their plan all prepared and were only waiting for some such un-expected occurrence as this to aid them, I cannot say; but they jumped at the op-portunity which had so suddenly arisen to rid them for a space of two of the five men against whom they had evidently laid some plot, and set about to over-power the rest of us. Of Chiffard they took little heed, apparently, although they lifted the remaining dory from the hatch and laid it quietly across the galley door, so that the cook would have a hard time of it getting out when he once became alarmed. Then they hurried to the companion-way, and our first intimation of trouble brewing was shouted down to us by Carquemort, who called upon Thatcher to come up on deck.

"What's the row?" returned Thatcher, somewhat surprised at the summons.

"No row," answered Carquemort; "the captain's just put off in a dory. Hurry up!"

We both rose to our feet to go on deck; but, as good fortune would have it, I, having slipped off my shoes when we came below, was delayed half a minute in putting them on again. That necessity, an insignificant thing in itself, probably saved the lives of four of us. Thatcher went on ahead, and in my inclined position I could follow him with my eyes until he stepped on the deck. No sooner had he

done so than an arm shot out from behind him, and he was struck in the back
of the head with a belaying-pin. Not a
sound did he make, but pitched forward
heavily and fell violently against the
wheel, where he lay motionless. For a
second I could not believe the testimony
of my own eyes; I thought he must have
slipped on the wet deck; but yet I had
seen the blow *struck*, and the sound of the
heavy fall of Thatcher's body was followed by absolute silence. If he had tumbled accidentally, Carquemort would be
assisting him to his feet. But there was
no evidence of that. All this flashed
through my mind in much less time than
it takes to write it, or even to read it, and
fearing treachery, I went at once to my
satchel that hung over my bunk and took
my revolver.

I had only just had time to make sure
it was loaded when I heard foot-falls on
the companion-way. I retired quickly to

the end of the cabin farthest from the steps and cocked my pistol. I thought I should have to deal with Carquemort, but to my surprise it was Semsen who faced me, the belaying-pin still in his hand.

"Don't you move another step!" I shouted to him, as his head appeared below the door-piece. I was leaning with my left hand upon the table and I had the drop on him with my right. The man seemed staggered at finding himself facing a revolver, for he hesitated a moment and raised his right hand as if to hurl the heavy pin at my head. Just then Carquemort shouted:

"Hurry up, you fool! They're putting about" (meaning the McLeods in the dory, I suppose).

"If you move, I'll shoot," said I; but Semsen must have had a small opinion of my marksmanship, for he made a leap from the steps towards me, and as he did so I fired.

He fell headlong upon the cabin floor. I knew he could not be fatally hurt, for I had aimed low, intending (like a fool) to hit him in the leg, so I leaped upon his prostrate form and pounded him upon the head as fiercely as I could with the butt of my pistol. This had the desired effect, for he lay like a log. The while I had kept a sharp eye on the door, but the sound of my shot must have knocked some of the temerity out of Carquemort, who, I am sure, had not the remotest suspicion that we carried fire-arms.

I did not know, of course, at this time that McLeod and Glen were away from the schooner; so I wondered what could possibly have happened to them, and very naturally conjectured that as they made no move to my assistance they must, for some reason, be powerless.

All this made me hesitate to climb the companion-way, and I delayed some moments in coming to my determination, which finally was to take the offensive at once. I fortified myself with a second pistol out of Thatcher's bag, and with both weapons cocked I made my way cautiously to the cabin door and peered carefully upward. There was no one to be seen, and not a sound to be heard above the dripping from the sails and shrouds. I crept slowly up the slippery steps, fearing at every moment to be attacked with a belaying-pin, but nothing of the kind befell; and when at last I stuck my head above the level of the companion-rail I saw Carquemort leaning over the bulwarks amidships, and consequently with his back to me. McLeod and Glen had just come along-side with the rescued dory, but, from where I watched, they were invisible to me, and I could form no idea of why Carquemort stood in that position.

After my shot in the cabin he had, no doubt, expected to hear sounds of a struggle, or, if Semsen were hurt, calls for assistance. But as neither followed he must have concluded that both of us were injured as a result of our collision, and that I, at least, was temporarily out of the fight. It was the better part of valor, too, for him to make no personal investigation into the conditions that held in the cabin ; for (as he had signalled to Semsen) the two McLeods had put about and were rapidly nearing the schooner. As matters stood, therefore, he was left single-handed to meet these two ; and, considering their approach a graver danger than my possible advance from out of the cabin, he had abandoned his post at the top of the companion - way and lay in wait for the unsuspecting Scotsmen. Of course, all this, let me repeat, was wholly without my knowledge and beyond my comprehension, and consequently I did not act with such alacrity as I might had I held any conception of the lay of affairs. My courage, too, was effectually sapped by the sight of Thatcher lying face downward upon the deck, not six feet distant, apparently dead, with an ugly gash above the ear, from which a little stream of blood spread into an ugly pool upon the planking.

I consider that the protrusion of my head above the companion-way rail and the arrival of McLeod and Glen alongside the *Merry Madge* were simultaneous. The skipper, being in the bow of the dory, and holding the painter in one hand, stood up and started to clamber over the rail amidships. As he did so, Carquemort leaped from the lounging position he held and caught McLeod full in the face with a belaying-pin. At the same instant I sprang to the deck, just in time to see the captain throw up his hands and fall backward. He struck the side of the dory with the small of his back and plunged head first into the sea, upsetting Glen into the water at the same time. But even before the splash of the falling men and Glen's sharp cry had reached my ears, I had fired twice at Carquemort—missing with both cartridges. He turned quickly upon me, and seizing another pin from the main rigging near which he stood, he made a step in my direction. I fired again, and this time the bullet struck him under the right arm, making only a slight flesh-wound a few inches below the shoulder-blade.

Chiffard had not heard the report of my first shot at Semsen in the cabin, but the shouts and the firing which followed my arrival on deck roused him in his galley, and even in the excitement of my encounter with Carquemort I could hear the cook cursing and struggling with the heavy dory that had been placed to bar his passage.

" Arm yourself, Chiffard !" I shouted. "Arm yourself !"—and hardly had I cried these words when Carquemort, with a savage oath, flew at me, dropping the heavy pin he held and drawing from his belt an ugly knife that I had frequently seen him use to cut tobacco. I did not wait for the onslaught, but turned and fled forward along the opposite side of the deck, thus placing the cabin skylight and the main-mast momentarily between me and my pursuer. I reached the galley just as Chiffard burst himself free and stepped on deck, holding in his hand a long meat-knife. I turned then, restored to some confidence by his presence, and faced Carquemort, who was now within less than five yards of us. I raised both my pistols and fired with the two at one time, and, thank God, hit the mark, for Carquemort fell prone forward with one bullet in the abdomen and another in his left wrist. These details of injury we did not make sure of until later, but we knew at once from the way he lay

I FIRED BOTH PISTOLS AT ONE TIME

writhing and cursing that he would give us no more trouble for the moment.

I had had no time to think of McLeod and Glen meanwhile, but as soon as we had made sure that Carquemort was safely hurt, I thrust the bewildered Chiffard towards the starboard rail, saying I know not what as I did so, and gazed keenly over the board. The two dories had floated some distance away, and close in to the schooner drifted an oil-skin cap— but no sign of either McLeod or Glen. Almost before I could make any comment, Chiffard seized me by the shoulder and pointed aft, and there, as the mainsail swung heavily to port, I saw Glen standing in the stern dripping wet, dressed only in shirt and trousers; and as my eyes fell upon him he leaped forward with a shout and seized a man who came up from the cabin. It was Semsen, of course, and I called this to Chiffard as we leaped over ropes and tackle to Glen's assistance.

The experiences I had passed through within the last half-hour had taken pretty nearly all the vigor out of me, so that it is not to be wondered at that Chiffard reached Glen in about the time it took me to cover half the distance. He got aft none too soon, however, for Semsen had rushed at the lad with a knife, and the two had grappled and fallen upon the slimy boards at the first shock, the murderous Finn on top. Chiffard was no man to ask questions at a time like this. He saw the steel flashing near Glen's throat, and without further ceremony he lunged forward and thrust his own meat-knife deep into the man's body just under the left arm, dealing what must have been instant death. And then, in his growing fury, as the Finn's grasp relaxed on the prostrate boy, Chiffard lifted the man bodily from the deck, poised him for a moment on the after guard-rail, and heaved him into the sea.

CHAPTER XXII

THE FATE OF THE *MERRY MADGE*

GLEN was still lying on the deck breathless and half stunned; but when he assured us he was not hurt, I turned towards Thatcher, calling upon Chiffard to assist. I felt almost certain that he was dead, but to our great joy his pulse was beating feebly, and his breath came heavily and in gasps when we turned him upon his back and propped his head on my coat, which I pulled off and rolled into a pillow. From the cabin I brought some brandy and forced it down his throat, and we chafed his hands and bathed his face until, after some ten minutes of this operation, he opened his eyes. Then we bandaged his head after such clumsy manner as we could, and made him as comfortable as possible on the deck. I wanted to carry him below, but the poor fellow raised his hands in such prayerful objection when we attempted to lift him that I sent the cook down for a mattress and a blanket, and we kept him above. For this let us again offer up our thanks to Providence!

We passed the brandy-bottle over to Glen, and a couple of good pulls at it revived the lad, who at once sat up and, to our questions, gave the facts that fill out this chapter of death with the events that concern him and his father.

When McLeod fell beneath Carquemort's coward blow he tumbled backward into the sea, and being weighted with rubber boots and a long oil-skin coat (and senseless, probably, besides), he sank at once. Glen was a good swimmer, and regained the schooner in two strokes after he had been thrown into the water by

the capsizing of the dory. He clambered upon the rail, and without waiting to
see what was going on aboard, threw off
his hat and shoes and dived after his father. The ice-cold water sent him quickly to the surface, however, half numbed,
and he pulled himself to the deck just
in time to be met by Semsen, who had
meanwhile come to his senses again in
the cabin. Under ordinary circumstances
the lad would have been a match for the
Finn, but half frozen as he was he fell
an easy mark to the latter's attack, and
would doubtless have proved another vic-
tim to the conspiracy if Chiffard had not
been so handy with his meat-knife.

All this time we could hear Carquemort cursing and groaning where he had
dropped before my lucky shots half an
hour before; and when we felt that all
had been done that was possible for
Thatcher and Glen, the latter being also
rolled in a blanket on the poop, Chiffard

and I went forward to see if we could do anything for the undeserving blackguard. If I had let him have his way, the cook would have sent the fellow to join Semsen; but I held him from this, and with little effort, after we had seen the wounds, for one of my bullets had torn clean through the man's body. Even while we did what little we could for him, the brute cursed and reviled us, and called out again and again, in his half-delirious raving, that we were now only two to divide the treasure—he thinking, doubtless, as I had thought, that Thatcher was dead. Presently, however, his bawling degenerated into a wordless muttering, and he soon fell unconscious. We carried him into the forecastle and did what we could to make him comfortable in his bunk, but that was not much.

During the excitement of the past hour none of us, of course, had paid the slightest heed to anything beyond the very pressing business at hand—our world being for the time bounded by the bulwarks of the *Merry Madge*—and consequently we had failed to hear the low moan of a fog-horn that must have been sending its warnings to us through the mist for a considerable period. But suddenly, as we came aft from the forecastle, we were called to a sense of our surroundings by a hoarse roar that seemed to burst out of the clouds. We were too startled to realize at first the direction whence the whistling had come, but we could judge from the tone that a great steamer must be within half a league of us. We rushed aft, where Glen had already jumped to his feet and was making a search for the tin horn. But there was no sign of it anywhere. Chiffard ran forward in the hope of finding it in the bow, and after what seemed an interminable period to our straining ears the fierce bellowing of the fog-monster roared again across the quiet sea. Not a breath of air stirred. The sails hung limp and useless, and even if there had been a breeze, I doubt if we could have done much towards escaping our fate. The cook came aft empty-handed, and again the steamer blew that awful note. This time we rushed to the starboard rail, and even poor Thatcher raised himself on his elbow. We felt as if the vessel could not be more than a hundred yards from us. God will that she might pass across our bows!

"Shout! All hands shout together!" cried Glen, and we threw our united voices into a desperate yell.

What a mockery! We might as well have tried to speak the land, and as our pygmy call died away we heard the throbbing of the oncoming propeller, as it churned full speed through the fog-bound sea. We stood like stone men, leaning upon the rail and waiting for the next whistle. But before it came, a great dark object

A GREAT DARK OBJECT ROSE UP OUT OF THE SEA

rose up out of the sea abeam and climbed high into the fog, like some huge ocean monster rearing itself to fall upon its prey. Terrified, we fell back, and with a bellowing roar of the whistle and a hissing of parting water the great iron steamship crashed into the *Merry Madge*, cutting her clean in two between the masts, and with a groaning and scraping of timbers, charged onward through the wreck and dove again into the thickness of the mist. We were all knocked from our feet as the schooner careened, and when the main-mast crashed into the foaming water astern of the steamship, that part of the schooner we lay on listed forward, and I just managed to seize Thatcher by the collar in time to save him from sliding into the whirlpool. When I looked up the steamer was beyond the scope of our vision, and not a sound came to us from her again. I had seen a man at her bow as she struck us, and I had seen him throw up his arms and turn towards the bridge, and probably he shouted, but any further sign of human life aboard our destroyer was not given to us. The liner rushed on through the fog, full speed, towards Europe, and apparently, for all her hundreds cared, Heaven might help the poor banks fishermen!

When we had in some measure recovered from the shock of our catastrophe, I saw that the four of us were clinging to the after half of the cloven schooner, yet in no immediate danger of death from drowning, for the sea was still calm. The stern of the *Merry Madge* was yet on almost an even keel, and the ripples washed gently up the slanting deck which now lay as an inclined plane rising abruptly out of the water from where the mainmast had formerly stood. Beyond, I could espy the forward half of the schooner, and I knew from the way it lay that the forecastle was well under water, and that Carquemort, therefore, was delivered of his sufferings. On the waves about us floated spars, hatches, casks, planks, and various kinds of wreckage; but there was one item of our cargo which I knew would never float again, and that was the gold which had laid piled in the cabin just forward of the main-mast, and must have plunged into Davy Jones's locker when the big stick was torn from its fastenings.

There was no word spoken by any one for a long space, as we all clung for life to the wreck. When at last we did come to speech our talk was foolish at the first, as the talk of men thrown out of one danger into the face of another is very likely to be. Yet from talk we turned presently to action, and lashed Thatcher to the wheel, for he was still but semiconscious, and far too weak to do anything for himself. We made lashings ready for ourselves, too, against the possibility of a rising wind. But even so, we felt the risk we were taking, for the hulk we clung to might fill at any moment, or suddenly keel over and go down.

Not far away, however, we caught sight of one of our dories, which seemed whole, and Glen, being already drenched, volunteered to swim to it and bring it back, we to keep hallooing to him should the mist thicken. Chiffard made ready to go to his assistance should he need it; but, fortunately, excitement lent power to the lad, and we saw him at last clamber safely into the boat, where he lay for some minutes almost exhausted. Then he paddled clumsily about, propelling his craft by the palms of his hands, and picked up two oars from the drift before he pulled back to us on the derelict.

We threw the mattress into the bottom of the boat and passed Thatcher over the rail, where the cautious Chiffard, who had put the brandy-bottle in his pocket, dosed the wounded man into a partial comfort again, and he fell off into a heavy sleep. I looked at my watch and found that it was now two o'clock in the afternoon. This concrete knowledge of the time of day brought us all to a realization of the hunger that was gnawing at our stomachs, and face to face with the still sterner fact that we had no provisions to satisfy this hunger, and probably would be unable to retrieve any from either portion of the wreck. Nevertheless, we determined upon an attempt, and Chiffard was deputed to row over to the bow in the dory and do what he could in the way of foraging. It seemed to Glen and me as though he were gone an hour or more, as we sat astraddle of the taffrail. But by the watch his expedition occupied him less than thirty minutes. In that time he collected two tins of biscuit and six bottles of red wine that had been stowed in the galley. He had managed to get these by cutting in through the galley skylight with a hatchet that he found in the chains. We made a poor meal off some of the biscuit and a bottle of the wine, but we felt somewhat cheered by the thought that starvation was at least twenty-four hours further away from us than had at first appeared.

The fog still hung heavy about us and no sound came to our ears, and by the time night fell we had floated out of sight of the other half of the *Merry Madge*, and hope hung heavy in our hearts. There was little sleep for any of us, although we took turns through the long night at lying with Thatcher in the bottom of the dory, while two watched on the wreck holding the painter in hand, for we dared not tie up to so precarious a buoy.

CHAPTER XXIII

A TREASURE LAUGHED AWAY

DURING the night we suffered considerably from the cold, and we dared not fortify ourselves with what was left of the brandy for fear of depriving Thatcher of further stimulant should he take a turn for the worse. But our sufferings fell, as our hopes rose, at about four o'clock— which must have been near dawn—for a light breeze ruffled the waters and seemed to whisper to us that the fog would lift; and we knew that if it did there was good chance of our being seen and rescued by some steamer, for we were apparently lying in the lane.

The wind increased as the daylight grew, and at sunrise the mist went tumbling off to westward, disclosing to our anxious gaze nothing but a rolling, empty sea, as calm and peaceful as if it had never known a tragedy. Nowhere in sight was the bow portion of the ill-fated *Merry Madge*, and we judged that it must have gone down in the night.

During those dark hours we had talked, Chiffard and I, of our great loss; and hope (clinging to a straw, as hope will) nursed for us the thought that at least the chest, which had been stowed in the port state-room, might still be above water, and safe, so long as the shattered stern floated. So great a hold did this idea obtain upon our minds that, as soon as we had breakfasted upon claret and biscuit, we started to cut a hole through the deck. Thatcher watched us eagerly from the dory, for he had rested well in the night and could now sit up and talk, suffering, however, from violent pains in the head.

The undertaking gave us occupation, at least, which was of benefit under the circumstances, and as we hacked away at the planks we felt within us a certain element of that old fever which had been upon us at the time we were rolling stones on the summit of La Grande Vigie. But the present was slow and difficult work for men more or less weak and exhausted, and the hatchet we labored with was a sorry tool indeed.

While one of us chopped the other two sat on the highest part of the rail and watched the horizon for a sail or for smoke, and it was during one of my tricks at deck-splitting that Glen gave a shout which brought us all to our feet and caused me in my excitement to let the hatchet slip from my hands into the sea, and almost to follow it myself. But the sight I was called to was worth the loss. A little brown film rested on the water far to the northeast, and from time to

time it darkened or melted almost entirely away.

" A steamer !" cried Glen.

" Can you tell how she's heading ?"
asked Thatcher, eagerly, for he was too
low down even to see the signs.

" Not yet," replied Glen, pulling off his
shirt; " but give me that oar and we'll try
to make them see us if they come this
way."

The smoke grew heavier and heavier,
and after half an hour of anxious gazing
we could see the mast - head of the approaching steamship. I cannot tell in
words how we felt when we became convinced that we lay near her probable
course, nor the sensation we experienced
as she became plainly visible, and how,
at length, when we had waved and waved
seemingly to no purpose, we saw white
puffs issue from the whistle, and presently heard the ship's answer to our signals.
She swerved in closer to the wreck, but

she seemed to take an eternity in plough-
ing through the water that separated us
from her. Finally, when she had. come
close enough for us to distinguish the
faces and forms of the men upon her
deck, she stopped and let down a boat.
Thatcher had spoken no word during all
this excitement, but when he saw the
boat lowered he said:

" Men, not a syllable to these fellows
about the fight. We were run down and
lost the captain and two hands. I got my
wound in the wrecking. Understand ?"

We nodded; but Chiffard said :

" And the chest ?"

" It's all right about the chest," answered Thatcher; " I'll ask the captain to help
us get it when we go aboard." And then
we turned towards the boat that was near
and cheered lustily for our rescuers.

They were good-hearted, rough fellows
who pulled us into the stern of their long-
boat, and the officer at the tiller pro-

duced a flask first thing. Briefly we told
of our experience, and I mentioned the
chest in the cabin.

"What's in it?" asked the officer.

"Money," I answered; "a good deal
of money, too."

He laughed, and the men followed in
loud guffaw.

"That's pretty good, too," continued
the officer. "A banker with a money-
chest! How long have you fellows been
without food? Better tell that yarn to
the captain. 'Way there!" he shouted,
and the sailors fell to their oars, laughing the while, for they thought us out of
our heads.

I saw it was of no use to say more
to the officer, and waited patiently until
we were brought to the ship, which was
the British tramp, *Dunkellen Castle*, Captain Christopher, in ballast from London
to New York. But there, too, a burly
captain laughed in our faces and winked

at his mate, and sent us all below to the cabin, where the cook had spread us a royal feast of meat and coffee, and while we were yet protesting and expostulating we heard the engine bell tinkle, and soon the ship was vibrating from stem to stern bearing us away forever from what little might have been left to us of those mill-ions we had seen and handled and owned. But now this is all past regrets.

They treated us well aboard the *Dunkellen Castle*, and the steward, who had some knowledge of broken heads, dressed Thatcher's wound for him daily, and by the time we got back to doctors he was well on towards recovery. We got plenty of rest and five nights of sound sleep, and on the afternoon of the sixth day the *Dunkellen Castle* dropped her anchor off Bedloe's Island.

No voyagers, I believe, were ever more grateful to see their home port, and when this page falls under the eyes of Captain

Christopher, of the *Dunkellen Castle*, if it ever does, he may feel that the men he rescued on the Newfoundland banks will always hold for him a long credit balance of gratitude.

CHAPTER XXIV

CONCLUSION.—THE YARN OF THE *NOTRE DAME*

IT were no doubt the part of wisdom to let the preceding chapter make an end to this narrative, for it completes the tale, and there is no more to be said concerning our adventures in that unfortunate summer of 1894. But we have been so taunted by the few intimates to whom we have related the incidents here set forth, that I cannot resist the temptation of casting defiance in their faces and of bidding them seek further evidence if they cannot take our words for the truth of it all.

These sceptics will find in the Canadian shipping list, if they will take the trouble to look, a record of the schooner *Merry Madge*, of North Sydney, McLeod, master, and of her loss at sea in the latter part of August, 1894.   They can also easily ascertain that Thatcher and I were in Halifax, Nova Scotia, on the dates given, and they may trace us to Sydney, where, I wager, the host of the Hôtel des Ambassadeurs still holds a memory of us.   That we were in St. Pierre may be easily proven, for we were looked upon as curiosities there, and I dare say there is more than one person to this day wondering how we ever got away from the island, for it must have seemed to them that we disappeared mysteriously.   And as to the truth of our rescue by the crew of the *Dunkellen Castle*, it is a simple affair to watch the shipping news in any New York daily paper, and, the next time the vessel comes to port, to go aboard of her and put plain questions to Captain Christopher.   The only assistance I must refuse to these investigators is the disclosure of the identity of our good friend Chiffard. But I may say that he no longer keeps on South Fifth Avenue. Madame moved the establishment while he was away, and I should be the last one to give their present address, for you will remember that Thatcher holds my promise.

As to the history of the treasure, that came to us quite unexpectedly in the spring-time of the following year, and from our old friend M. de Manclay, who was *de passage* in New York on his way to Europe with his family. We found him by chance at the little French hotel in University Place, and he was apparently overjoyed at seeing us. He would have none of our refusals to dine with him, and over the courses he talked and talked as was his delight, and spun yarn after yarn from the wealth of his memories!

Out of pure recklessness, I believe, Thatcher asked him if he had ever heard of buried treasure in Miquelon, and to our unbounded amazement he replied that he had, and at once riveted our attention by saying that St. Pierre, like almost every other island along the Atlantic coast, has its fable of hidden gold.

I will not attempt to go into the fulness of the story as told by our garrulous friend, for the essence of it is sufficient to our purpose, and the facts in brief are these. (We have verified them since from the archives of the Ministère de la Marine et des Colonies, in Paris.)

In 1744, three French ships, the *Louis Érasme*, the *Marquis d'Antin*, and *Notre Dame de la Délivrance* (cf. the lettering on the lid of the strong box!) set sail from Callao, Peru, with a vast amount of treasure concealed under a surface cargo of cocoa. Off the Azores the Frenchmen fell in with the British privateers, *Duke* and *Prince Frederick*, and after a three-hours' fight the *Louis Érasme* and the *Marquis d'Antin* were captured. In the smoke and the excitement of the action the *Notre Dame de la Délivrance* made good her escape. Her captain, not daring to approach the French coast lest he likewise fall a prey to the enemy, whose privateers were cruising about that region in great numbers, crowded on all sail and laid his course for Louisburg, then in the possession of the French King. In about twenty days the *Notre Dame* sighted Scatary, and her captain must have thought his treasure saved; but, as ill luck would have it, he fell in with the British ships *Sunderland, Boston,* and *Chester.* When they sighted the enemy from the tops, the French were close in to a fleet of cod fishermen from St. Pierre. The captain hailed one of the bankers and conceived the idea of dividing the risk, by transshipping half of his precious cargo. This task he accomplished in little more than an hour, and as the wind was light the British fleet had made but a small approach when the *Notre Dame* finally hoisted all sail in flight. But she was eventually captured, and the crews of the *Chester*, *Boston*, and *Sunderland* got great prize - money — over $4,000,000 in bars of gold being taken with the *Notre Dame*. Rumor has it that the fishermen made St. Pierre in safety, and buried the treasure somewhere on the island. " But," said M. De Manclay, confidently, " I have small faith in such a possibility—else some record must have been made of this fact. The schooner was lost in the sea, or captured by the enemy—which is the more likely—and that was an end of it, *voilà tout !*"

" And you say half the *Notre Dame's* treasure was thrown aboard the fishing-boat ?" asked Thatcher.

" So the story goes."

" Then the fishermen carried as much as the ship—four million dollars ?"

"It is well possible," said M. de Manclay, laughing. "The larger the figure, the greater the romance, eh?"

"And the gold has never been found?" I asked, ingenuously.

"No; nor will be," said the old Frenchman.

"Has no treasure ever been dug up on the island?"

"Not that I ever heard of," answered the old gentleman. "And had there been I should have known of it. News of that kind travels fast."

I did not feel quite so sure about that. And perhaps M. de Manclay will change his mind if he will send some one to the top of La Grande Vigie to report to him upon the empty pit twenty-five paces from the summit.

THE END

By JAMES BARNES

A LOYAL TRAITOR. A Story of the War of 1812. Illustrated. Post 8vo, Cloth, Ornamental, $1 50.

A vigorous romance it is, full of life and adventure.—*N. Y. Herald.*

A stirring story. . . . The several characters are finely balanced and well drawn, and are admirably interwoven to give reasonableness and completeness in every chapter.—*Chicago Inter-Ocean.*

We turn with a feeling of relief to Mr. Barnes's breezy and Marryat-like story of the American privateersman. . . . This is all genuine romance, with a wide horizon and many changes of scene. . . . Mr. Barnes has done his work well.—*N. Y. Times.*

An excellent and intensely interesting story of romance and adventure.—*Brooklyn Standard-Union.*

The book has freshness, animation, and strong story-interest. —*Outlook, N. Y.*

A quick-moving, picturesque story. The daring Yankee sailor of that naval war, his life above deck and below, in battle and in cruise, his dialect and yarns, are all quaintly reproduced in a series of vivid scenes.—*Philadelphia Record.*

FOR KING OR COUNTRY. A Story of the American Revolution. Illustrated. Post 8vo, Cloth, Ornamental, $1 50.

NAVAL ACTIONS OF THE WAR OF 1812. Illustrated. 8vo, Cloth, Ornamental, $4 50.

NEW YORK AND LONDON

HARPER & BROTHERS, Publishers

By HOWARD PYLE

MEN OF IRON. Illustrated by the Author. 8vo, Cloth, Ornamental, $2 00.

TWILIGHT LAND. Illustrated by the Author. 8vo, Half Leather, $2 50.

A MODERN ALADDIN; or, The Wonderful Adventures of Oliver Munier. An Extravaganza in Four Acts. Illustrated by the Author. Post 8vo, Cloth, Ornamental, $1 25.

THE WONDER CLOCK; or, Four-and-Twenty Marvellous Tales: being One for each Hour of the Day. Illustrated by the Author. Embellished with Verses by KATHARINE PYLE. Large 8vo, Ornamental, Half Leather, $3 00.

THE ROSE OF PARADISE. Being a Detailed Account of Certain Adventures that happened to Captain John Mackra, in Connection with the famous Pirate, Edward England, in the Year 1720, off the Island of Juanna, in the Mozambique Channel, writ by himself, and now for the first time published. Illustrated by the Author. Post 8vo, Ornamental Cloth, $1 25.

PEPPER AND SALT; or, Seasoning for Young Folk. Superbly Illustrated by the Author. (*New Edition*). 4to, Ornamental Cloth, $1 50.

NEW YORK AND LONDON :

HARPER & BROTHERS, PUBLISHERS

☞ *The above works are for sale by all booksellers, or will be sent by the publishers, postage prepaid, on receipt of the price.*
3626

9 783337 026073